RENEGADE COPS

CROSS

ATLANTIC

FIASCO

An Original Story

By

PROLIFIC, INTERNATIONAL
BESTSELLING
AUTHOR
JOHN A. ANDREWS
CREATOR OF
THE RUDE BUAY SERIES
&
THE WHODUNIT CHRONICLES

11/19/16

Published in the U.S.A. by
BooksThatWillEnhanceYourLife

A L I
Andrews Leadership International
www.JohnAAndrews.com

ISBN: 9780984898046
Cover Design: ALI
Cover Photo: Anthony Johnson
Edited by: Harminder Kaur

RENEGADE COPS

A mission that only one man can fulfill…

"The woods are lovely, dark, and deep, But I have promises to keep, and miles to go before I sleep,"

Robert Frost

RENEGADE

COPS

TABLE OF CONTENTS

1

A YELLOW TAXI PULLS UP OUTSIDE a junk yard in nearby Culver City. The hanging high outside sign on the dark brown wooden building reads: JUNK CARS WANTED TOP $$$.

Vanessa Cox, Bill Levy and Robert Coles all ex-police officers of the Beverly Hills Police Department step out and mosey into the establishment. The Cab drives off making a U-turn.

A tall Hispanic man in his mid-50s adorned in brown greased stained coveralls approaches the trio and greets. He is chewing hard on the tobacco in his mouth. Before continuing, he then spits out the watery residue on the paved landing.

"What can we help you find today?"

He asks forcing a smile.

Vanessa Cox hands him a sheet of paper after unfolding it. The paper handling process unnerves him. Anyway, he reads its contents and then quickly radios one of his underlings.

A mud covered white Ford Crew Cab pickup truck calculatingly riding the bumps on the road emerges towards the wooded office. The brown spotted on white jalopy's front fenders are partially hanging onto the vehicle's front end.

The three ex-police officers board the jalopy. Vanessa Cox occupies the front passenger's seat and Bill Levy and Robert Coles in the rear cab.

Finally, after avoiding numerous mud filled pot holes, the pickup arrives on a hill overlooking a mountain of junked cars. Cox, Levy, and Coles disembark and follow the driver down a narrow track to where a tractor is methodically stacking multiple junk cars.

On top of the pile is a totaled black-and-white police cruiser, a Ford LTD. It bears the number "150" on its roof and trunk etched with a thick Futura Black typeface. Immediately Vanessa points to it with a great degree of confidence.

The driver of the pickup instructs the driver of the tractor to fetch the cruiser 150. He does and hoists it before dropping it on the pavement in front of the three ex-police officers. The trio begins inspecting it, led by Vanessa.

The rear tires of Cruiser 150 are still intact. Although its front end is a wreck, the front tires, and the front and rear windscreens are also missing.

Vanessa tries opening the driver's door of the wreck. It remains jammed. After a few tries, she gets it to open halfway amidst a squeaking sound. Vanessa looks inside. She is ecstatic.

Among the broken glass and debris, she notices a half pair of hooped gold earrings lying upon the floor. She picks up the single hoop earring and idolizes it. She reflects. She then puts it in her purse. Her partners in crime share with her an empathetic glance.

Vanessa reflects on being pulled out of that car during the day of the tragic accident. She opens her purse and quickly stashes away the piece of jewelry.

The female ex-cop is energized and toughens up. She authoritatively signals to open up the hood. The driver of the tractor obliges. After many tries, he manages to pry the hood open. Looking at the engine, it's covered with grime and dirt, but still pretty much intact. Vanessa smilingly surveys the motor. She likes what she sees under that hood: That robust eight-cylinder motor just in need of an engine wash almost barks at her in her imagination.

Looking at the Driver,

Bill Levy asks,

"How much?"

The driver, very surprised that they are making him an offer for the entire wreck, addresses Levy in Spanish.

"¿Cómo Señor?"

"Quanto?" reiterate Levy and Cox.

"Va a costar doscientos dólares,"

The driver replies.

Levy shells out two hundred and fifty dollars. He gives it to the driver. Additionally, he hands him a piece of paper, on it is a written address for Al's Shop.

"Drop it off there!"

States Levy.

The driver smiles, they climb back up the hill and board the pickup truck. The pickup departs while the tractor loads the cruiser onto a newly arrived flatbed tow truck.

2

AS THE THREE EX-POLICE OFFICERS return to the valley of the junkyard. Vanessa once again entangled, reflecting on the fatal accident which almost took her life.

Several months prior to this junkyard visit, gunshots rang out at a quiet apartment complex in Beverly Hills, California. Moments later, two Hispanic men in their mid-20s discarded their weapons inside a resident dumpster. Subsequently, they flee the premises at high speed in a red Toyota pickup truck.

The alerted neighbors, after hearing the gunshots immediately call 911. The Beverly Hills Police dispatched several officers to the scene. Meanwhile, the pickup merged with traffic on local streets heading towards Los Angeles.

Officer Vanessa Cox had just been given the keys to a brand-new Ford LTD by her boss John Croft and was fetching a soda at the local Seven Eleven on Melrose Avenue. Vanessa gets the call and races to the crime scene. She is the first of officers to arrive. The officer is surrounded by flustered residents who heard the gunshots. They point her to the unit where the shots allegedly came from. She secures the crime area and seals it off from the neighbors. She then races upstairs to the apartment unit in an investigative pursuit.

Upon arriving, she notices a middle-aged Caucasian woman lying face up in a blood bath with gunshot wounds to her upper torso. The victim is lifeless. Additionally, Cox clues in on the ransacked dwelling with the bed mattress tossed one side, the bedroom dresser draws ajar, and cupboard and medicine cabinets opened. In the bathroom, she discovers a disheveled purse with no money inside it, opened clothes closet with clothing on hangers lying upon the floor. The officer senses a brutal robbery to which she has been dispatched. The scene is so despicable; Cox vomits up the half can of soda she had consumed. Finally, she pulls herself together.

By this time, additional police officers arrived at the scene. Cox quickly dispatched them throughout the neighborhood to find out who else had seen or heard anything about the shooting incident. Moments later, word came back that a woman after the sound of a gunshot, saw a red pickup truck speeding up her block, though she wasn't sure if the vehicle had anything to do with the crime. That was all she knew.

Meanwhile, miles away the red pickup is heading speedily for a getaway into Los Angeles. It merges with traffic heading west on the 10 freeway at continued high speed.

Another call comes in over Vanessa's radio. "Red pickup truck spotted on the 10 freeway weaving in and out of traffic erratically with two unidentified men." Vanessa looks to the other newly arrived officers.

"You all got this, right? I have got to catch those bastards."

Says Vanessa Cox,

"What evidence have you gathered thus far?"

Asks one officer,

"As far as I could tell it looks like a fatal robbery. That's a given. I have dispatched officers throughout the neighborhood. Look for additional evidence. I've got to be on this chase. Plus I need to break in 150."

"How about backup?"

She doesn't respond.

Vanessa barges out.

She re-boards the police Cruiser 150. Turns on the ignition revs up the engine and leaves the apartment parking lot at high speed. Moments later, she merges with traffic on the 10 freeway westbound driving the brand-new Ford LTD vehicle. Sirens and flashing lights welcome this vehicle to the freeway. Weaving in and out of traffic Vanessa Cox is in pursuit of the perpetrators driving that red pickup truck. She finally lands the HOV lane as other vehicles give-way.

Miles up ahead, Vanessa sees the red pickup bobbing and weaving out of traffic. She speeds up and moments later finds herself a few car lengths behind the pickup. The driver of the pickup truck senses not only being tailed by one police car but his look into the rearview mirror indicates that a fleet of cruisers is now closing in behind the lead car in the high-speed chase.

The pickup truck takes the Crenshaw Boulevard exit attempting a getaway. A cargo van, almost missing the exit, from the left lane slices its way behind the pickup truck.

Vanessa, unable to slow down at such a high speed, slams into the van rear-ending it. Other police cars in the chase manage to stop abruptly. Even so, the van blocks the entrance to the exit ramp upon colliding with the cruiser. Therefore, the chase abruptly comes to a halt. As a result, not only does the pickup truck elude them but Vanessa suffers bruises about the head along with minor concussions. Moments later, Paramedics arrive at the scene. With the help of other officers, they drag her out of the wreck.

3

ALMOST ONE YEAR AFTER THE accident and just nine days before Christmas, Vanessa Cox answers her apartment door. She was up most of the night talking over the phone with Levy and Coles about her tenure and attraction with Cruiser 150. The coffee pot is empty except for sediments. She drank all the coffee in the teacup which sits next to the sugar bowl and a can containing coffee creamer. Looking up at the clock, she realizes it's now mid-morning.

The UPS driver delivers her a package. After signing for it, she opens it and discovers a set of Ford's keys. She recognizes the set of keys. The only thing different on the ring is: there is a tag which reads: AL's

NINE DAYS LATER, it is Christmas Eve. The sound of bagpipes fills the air, soothing the hurry-up and going-nowhere-fast motorists. A motorbike at the stop light reminds everyone that it is a jolly good time of the year. The revelry is a high-octane performance. The house music medley blasts loudly from that two wheeler's twin speakers – one on either side of the vehicle just like a serenade on wheels.

A police officer directing traffic outside the Beverly Center confronts, and asks a bus operator to vacate the taxi stand, claiming that his vehicle has been standing there way too long. The bus driver accommodates.

Shoppers at the mall are busy catching up on their last minute Christmas shopping. In the lobby, there is a long line of shoppers waiting to get their presents wrapped by an elderly couple. With every adhering of a ribbon, the couple says: "Merry Christmas."

Outside Bill Levy's condo, a yellow cab pulls up and waits. Levy comes out carrying a duffel bag. He is police uniformed, wearing a badge which reads: Frank Chavez. The cab drives off.

Bill Levy reflects on the last time he wore the Beverly Hill's finest uniform. Which, ironically was that Monday after being grilled by Croft and Davis and calling it quits. Additionally, he recounts the day he received that last promotion and was asked to join Robert Coles and Vanessa Cox as part of a drug clean up task-force.

Prior to his promotion, Bill Levy one night was dispatched to a home on Sunset Boulevard in Beverly Hills. The calls came in from some suspicious neighbors who had seen multiple vehicles drop by at a house across the street. According to them, the motorists entered the house and then left after a few minutes. They suspected they were buying drugs as the house had that kind of activity 24/7.

When Bill Levy arrived, a motorist had just gotten back in his car and taken off. Bill followed the car and pulled it over a few blocks away. After a routine check, Bill realized that the driver, a 30-year-old Hispanic male was wanted in an unsolved hit and run accident which left the other motorist paralyzed. His department had been trying to solve this crime for over five years.

Bill Levy placed handcuffs on the man. After searching his car, he discovered in its' trunk over 5 kilos of uncut cocaine. Bill called in for backup. When the other officers arrived, they transported the arrested man to the Beverly Hills Police Station.

Bill returned to the resident in question. After ringing the doorbell and announcing himself, a Caucasian man in his 60s responded. Levy told him he was informed drugs were being sold off the premises. The man denied any involvement. Backup officers were now on the scene. Bill persisted and eventually ended up searching the house.

As a result of the search, over 15 kilos of uncut cocaine was confiscated in addition to several handguns, and a duffel bag stuffed with twenty-dollar bills. It was also discovered that the man was wanted in Las Vegas for the shooting death of a bouncer at the Boulevard Nightclub.

The Police department praised Bill for his persistence in talking the elderly man into a search on the premises. They later dubbed Bill Levy as Two in One Night.

THE CAB later picks Coles at his house. Robert Coles is also police-uniformed, wearing a badge which reads: Harry Bates, and carrying a small bag. He gets in and greets Bill Levy. The cab drives off. Both men are very upbeat about their mission. Even so, they keep their silence.

Meanwhile, Robert Coles reflects on the first day he teamed up with Bill Levy and fast driving Vanessa Cox.

Robert Coles like John Croft were detective specialists. Robert came on board at Beverly Hills from the Watts Police Department. He became an understudy of John Croft.

The Beverly Hills Department had been working on an unsolved rape case for over three years. Although they had made several arrests, none of them seemed to hold any weight. They had recently picked up a 30-year-old Caucasian man named Mike, but they couldn't find enough evidence to convict him of the crime. The man had been involved in a previous rape charge but ended up walking scot free.

Coles was an aggressive detective; coming in from Watts and being under the tutelage of Croft. The department handed the case over to him to see if he could crack it.

The first day at it, Coles went over to the jail and interrogated the alleged offender for several hours without getting a confession. Coles was willing to persist because it was discovered that the man attended a nightclub regularly in the area where the victim a 25-year-old brunette worked the graveyard shift.

DNA samples of Mike were being tested. On the following day, Coles returned to the interrogation room and told Mike straight up that his DNA matched. Mike was confused about this entire ordeal. Coles fabricating the results told Mike it was a match. Mike was led into a confession to the crime. Mike broke down in tears, as he spilled his guts, about waiting until the victim got off from work one early morning. He admitted that night he had several drinks more than usual. The DNA was released but remained sketchy. Mike had anyway already confessed that he did it.

The police department liked that aggressive attitude and paired Coles up with some top brass in Levy and Vanessa Cox.

DETECTIVE CROFT, HIS WIFE Elizabeth, along with their three daughters, Tamara 12, Denise 11 and Brianna 9 are enjoying the day before Christmas shopping spree at the Beverly Center. They are immediately sucked into the crowd of the mall as customers couldn't avoid soft collisions with each other. The Croft family adjusts and accommodates, showing some spirit of Christmas courtesy. In their view, the mall traffic mirrors the pedestrian traffic on 34th and 42nd streets in New York City. They have been there and jokingly turned many pedestrians away.

Vanessa Cox gets out of a taxicab and strolls inside the Al's Chop Shop. She is the alias Tess Shoemaker.

Inside the other taxi, Coles and Levy leaf through a day planner and contemplate. Suddenly, the cabin which they ride is stuck in gridlock traffic. This traffic jam now resembles a Friday evening Los Angeles multiplied by ten or a busy parking lot. Although, the time says it is still only mid-afternoon, on the alphanumeric numbered lettered clock on the dash of the taxi cab. The two ex-police officers, though anxious show signs of impatience with the continuous stop and go rush-hour traffic.

In the interim, at the Chop Shop, Vanessa gets inside the Cruiser 150, turns the engine and revs it up. She likes the sound from the motor. She drives away stoked.

The taxi pulls up outside First Nations Bank. At the end of the busy cul-de-sac, it double-parks.

Coles and Levy exit and enter the bank.

The driver of the car parked parallel to the taxi enters his car immediately after exiting the bank. The car drives off. The taxi cab driver sees the Cruiser coming from inside his rearview mirror. He buckles up and drives away cautiously.

Cruiser 150 pulls up right into the vacant spot. Inside this refurbished car, Vanessa Cox waits. She's busily applying makeup. The face powder spills onto the front passenger seat. She tidies up and wishes that this is a sign of good luck.

Meanwhile, inside the bank, Levy talks with a teller at her counter. While Robert Coles converses with the East Indian security guard close to the entrance door. Coles questions the guard,

"Any problems today, sir? I thought I heard someone say that there was a minor incident or something?"

The security guard replies in a thick Indian dialect,

"Not to my knowing. Everything today? …Copacetic! Very *copacetic!*"

"False alarm I guess, these have been frequent."

Replies Robert Coles.

Levy is working his game. He leans in towards the bank teller at the window and addresses her,

"… I would like to access my safety deposit box."

"What is your number?"

The teller asks.

"1734"

Replies Levy.

The teller, a Hispanic woman in her early 20s leaves and returns with a signature ledger.

Levy signs the name Frank Chavez. To the teller, it is a match.

The Yuppie bank manager, dressed in a khaki brown suit, a white shirt, and a bright yellow shirt takes over from the teller. His name tag reads Ralph Gomez. Ralph steps up and escorts Levy through a door to the bank's inner quarters. Now inside, he asks Levy for the matching safety deposit box key. Levy reaches inside his jacket and pulls out an automatic weapon.

Bill Levy had always wanted to rip off a bank. Even during his tenure as one of Beverly Hill's finest. Bill thought about it every time he visited the bank but refrained; fearing it would ruin his career. His career was over. And now, he was not only in the middle of his wish coming true. In fact, it could be one of the biggest bank robberies in history if the armored truck did not pick up yet, as he anticipated. To him, it was all or nothing. It was his chance to *get filthy, hog-nasty, stinking dirty rich*. Finally, he could buy his own island and have his own police force if the vault had enough money inside of it.

"Screw the Beverly Hills Police Department!"

He said to himself,

"All the way to the vault ... Ralphie!"

Says Levy with his pointed gun on him.

Ralph Gomez not ready for this is flustered and unraveled. So he hesitates.

Levy lets Ralph smell the sulfur at the tip of his gun. After, ensuring that Ralph has had a strong long whiff, Levy repeats himself.

"The vault...you hear me?"

Levy follows.

Ralph Gomez quickly locates the vault.

"Open it!"

Levy says,

"I can't,"

Says Ralph Gomez.

"What do you mean that you can't? What's the combination? You are pissing me off. I'm going to have to..."

Levy threatens.

Gomez's brown trousers turn browner as his embarrassment catches up to his timidity. His urine trickles down his trousers and onto the floor.

"I forgot it."

States Gomez.

"Think, recall bozo!"

Says Levy as he hits Gomez upside the head with the gun.

Gomez opens the vault.

Levy throws two sacks at him demandingly,

"Load them up and be quick about it."

Gomez fills up one sack with stacks of crisp twenty dollar bills. The other sack he fills with smaller bills, jewelry, and other documents from emptied safe deposit boxes.

"Now down on your knees,"

Orders Levy.

With Ralph Gomez in the kneeling, prayer position, Levy unties and yanks the yellow tie from around Gomez's neck and ties him up with his hands behind his back. Bill Levy leaves closing the two doors behind him.

5

LEVY RETURNS SPEEDILY TO the main area of the bank waving his pointed gun. He gets the attention of not only the bankers but the frazzled customers as well. He yells out!

"Hands on top of your head and get down low, and … nobody moves, or you get killed!" Levy checks the clock upon the wall opposite the entrance to the bank. He realizes that they have got to get out of there

ASAP without any flaws. Things have got to speed up if they are going to be able to pull this off successfully. He eyes his partner Robert Coles.

Quickly, Robert Coles steps up to the teller's window; while Levy keeps everyone at bay. Coles throws one sack to teller numbers one and two. Looking at them both, he orders:

"Fill them up, clean out everything. Come on move it!"

Teller number one tries to reach for the alarm alert button situated underneath her counter. Coles catches her in the act.

"Don't make me blow your hand off. I said to fill up the sack."

He continues,

"Step on it…"

The nervous crowd is not only restless but agitated and desperately wants to retaliate. This prolonged takeover of the bank by two men has given them a chance to figure out some vengeful tactics. In the crowd, an elderly woman removes her tired hands from the top over her head.

Levy sees her and aims to shoot her.

"Sir, could you please let my husband, and I go? We served in the Vietnam War and in Iraq. We don't want to be in another one of these things...My husband wears a purple heart to his country. I ..."

The woman pleads.

Levy interrupts.

"I said nobody moves! Are your hearing aids malfunctioning or need a new battery? Don't make me have to cap you..."

Sensing his seriousness the woman retreats to her husband's side.

Bill Levy oversees the filling of the last sack. Their mindset is to clean the house, thus leaving the bank cash empty. While Robert Coles grabs the filled sack from the teller number two and moves towards the guarding of the front door. The security guard tries escaping. Coles catches him in the act and trips him. Coles grabs the security guard's handcuffs located at the rear of his pants waist and places them on the security guard.

Outside Vanessa is poised inside the Cruiser 150 as it idles. She surveys, looking for any intruders to terminate. Her gun is a silencer ready.

Inside the bank teller number, one tries to activate the alarm for the second time.

Bill Levy notices and aims at her head.

She refrains.

Tension mounts as more weary aching hands of many on the floor remain raised above their head. Inside the crowd are two tellers who vacated their posts prior to the holdup of the bank by Coles and Levy. They are nervously sweating bricks as the two bank robbing ex-police officers are still in control.

The final sack is now filled with money. Bill Levy collects it. He briskly dashes for the exit door joining Robert Coles. Both men still maintain control of everyone inside the bank before making their exit.

On the outside, an armored truck pulls up and "double parks" in the cul-de-sac. The clock has been ticking for some time now. This is not the kind of situation Vanessa wanted to be involved in. She hates the midnight hour affair. "Give a woman time to think this getaway through," She thinks of the inside. Armored personnel steps out of the truck. Luckily, Levy and Coles come through the door. There is enough distraction for her to quickly dump two rounds in one of the armored men's body. Before Bill Levy can get to him, Vanessa cuts him down the bulletproof truck personnel with one round.

The armored truck driver attempts to fight back but has not even a chance to train his weapon, as bullets from Vanessa's rifle lays him flat in the street. Levy immediately sizes up the situation. With the two dead bodies on the ground, he glances at Coles. They toss their sacks of cash inside the cruiser on the rear seat.

Vanessa returns to the cruiser and positions the vehicle for the getaway.

"Door Jam!"

Yells Bill Levy,

Robert Coles clues in. He rushes towards the two corpses. Together they drag the two dead bodies up against the bank's front door.

They return hastily to the armored truck.

Levy goes inside the truck and begins to unload bags of cash. He tosses multiple mini sacks of cash to Robert Coles. Coles catches them. Vanessa pops open the cruiser's trunk. Coles tosses the small stacks of money into the trunk. He closes it securely.

In the interim, inside the bank, the nervous teller finally musters up enough courage to activate the alarm. Rattled and discombobulated customers regain their presence of mind. The alarm in the banks goes off. Several people inside the bank now rush towards the front door. Some push against it to no avail. They are trapped by the closed door.

Sirens are heard, in the distance, signaling the approach of oncoming law enforcement.

The armored truck's door is left ajar as Coles and Levy dash towards the cruiser to make their getaway.

Time is of the essence more than ever. They hustle.
Vanessa shifts the vehicle into the drive.
Both men hop inside and barely make it.
Cruiser150 takes off speedily with both rear doors still ajar. The doors slammed shut as the cruiser races over the speed bump.

INSIDE THE CAR, BILL LEVY, Robert Coles and Vanessa Cox are elated yet frazzled. They have their cash but realize that they are still in the wilderness segment of their getaway. Sirens echo in the distance.

Inside the bank, patrons, aided by bank personnel managed to push the door open, and heaves the corpses on the outside to one side.

They now congregate outside the bank. Noticing who kept the door closed, they are drained.

Meanwhile, Cruiser 150 weaves its way through the thickness of traffic.

The traffic light at the intersection turns yellow followed by a quick red, Cruiser 150 proceeds anyway. Moving vehicles brake avoiding the mayhem while the sounds of horns communicate disgust by those motorists. The Cruiser runs through the second, the third and fourth red traffic signal continuously. The next signal turns red at a busier intersection and several cars are now ahead of Cruiser 150. There's no way out. So it takes the sidewalk uprooting a water hydrant in its route.

Now the street is flooded with water. The Cruiser turns right onto a narrow two-way street. Vanessa navigates her way out of that two-way street traffic by forcing several yellow cabs to the curb. The cruiser heads for its getaway.

Meanwhile, more than a mile away at the Beverly Center, the Croft family is shopping bags laden. Brianna their nine-year-old daughter sees a Barbie Doll and wants it.

"Barbie! Barbie! Barbie! Can I have her?"
She yells.
"You have enough toys, sweetie."
Her mom, Elizabeth Croft assures.

"I will make her a new dress, lots of dresses. Come on mom, can I have her? We can play house together."
Brianna frowningly insists.
"Get it for her,"
Her dad instructs.
Elizabeth, already *shopped until she dropped* returns to purchase Brianna's cherished item.
In the interim, Croft's radio transmits:
"Bank robbery at Wilshire and La Cienega... robbers made their getaway in a Ford LTD police car. First Nations Bank! Two policemen and a getaway driver fled the scene of the robbery a few minutes ago. Two men from an Armored Truck were left dead at the scene."
Croft looks at his wife Elizabeth.
"Got to go Liz; serious police business. See you girls. I'll be home for Christmas."
He kisses his wife and three daughters. Then he races through the mall and scurries down the stairs on the La Cienega Blvd side to the building.
Downstairs and onto the street, he runs into the Traffic Police officer issuing a parking ticket. Croft flashes his badge. The officer acknowledges and accommodates.
Traffic is now at a complete stand still. Sirens reverberate.

Anyway, Croft darts in the rear seat of the Traffic Police's Chevy Blazer.

Inside the mall, Brianna admires the Barbie on display while her absentminded mom pays for the one just delivered to her by the salesperson.

The driver of the bus parked on outside the mall, now inside sizes up the situation and grabs Brianna. He picks her up, covers her mouth, and sticks an inhaler up to her nostrils.

The inhaled dosage instantly puts Brianna to sleep. Elizabeth and her other two daughters age 14 and 12, yell and pursue in vain. The bus driver eludes them.

Again, Elizabeth yells.

"My daughter, he snatched her from me. Somebody help... Help! "

It seems like the ones who would lend a hand is more occupied with the chase of Cruiser 150 on the mall's giant-sized plasma screen TV. By the time they get focused on the tragedy next to them and are ready to do the Great Samaritan deed, the bus driver along with his accompanying kidnapping partner has already boarded the parked bus across the street on San Vicente Blvd. The bus takes off with Brianna.

The bus travels in the opposite direction of the gridlocked traffic on La Cienega and on to Third Street, speedily heading west. With Brianna now asleep the associated kidnapper blindfolds her and tapes up her mouth.

Less than a mile away, several fender benders crowd the already busy street as a result of the velocity of Cruiser 150, now eluding a pursuing Beverly Hills Police SUV. Overhead helicopters pursue.

Running several red traffic signals consecutively, the cruiser makes its getaway as the SUV slams into a fire engine at the busy intersection. On impact, both vehicles explode sending flames onto the low-flying police and news- reporting-helicopters. They explode, bringing fire and debris onto the streets and like a ripple effect many vehicles are scorched, exploding into the air.

A few blocks away the Chevy Blazer remains stuck in traffic. Croft is peeved as it seems like there is no way out for him. The gridlock continues with numerous horns blowing and siren's blast.

7

DETECTIVE JOHN CROFT SEES a red slow moving Mustang. He jumps out of the Chevy Blazer. In the confrontation, he flashes his badge to the Hispanic driver of that speedster. The driver looks like he's in his early twenties.

"Need to borrow your car, police business!"
Croft states:

The driver hesitates.

"Didn't you hear me? I said..., police business!" Croft reiterates.

"That's not my business bro! I am the one who pays the note on this every month, plus insurance."

The driver replies.

"It's your business. BTW, this car smells like chronic...weed. You've been smoking weed and driving under the influence. You want to do some serious time for...?"

The Hispanic man steps out abandoning the hot rod. Croft jumps inside the vacant car and takes off in hot pursuit avoiding the inferno and fire trucks. He races the hot rod through the Beverly Hills and Santa Monica streets.

A FEW MILES UP ON PACIFIC COAST HIGHWAY Detective Croft spots Cruiser 150 as it turns the corner. Even so, as he notices the gas gauge inside the dashboard, Croft realizes that there's very little gas left in the tank. He pulls into the Shell Service Station. He notices a parked Sherriff car. Croft summons his assistance. The officer acknowledges him.

"We are with you."

The response comes back from Sheriff Scott, who abandons the purchasing a donut and coffee assignment at the Shell service station. Scott continues,

"Is your daughter also in that getaway car?"

Sherriff Scott asks as he jumps into his car leaving its door ajar.

Croft quickly does the refilling of the Mustang.

"Why should she?"

Croft asks.

"Your daughter Brianna is reported missing. Didn't you hear the news? You didn't get the phone call, detective?"

Croft checks for his cell phone. He doesn't have his cellular phone.

Croft completes filling up and takes off in order to catch up with Cruiser 150.

Meanwhile, back at the Beverly Center and inside the parked Chevy Blazer, on the rear-seat Croft's cell phone keeps on ringing. His mailbox is full. The traffic police officer is busy directing traffic. He has no idea that a phone is ringing in that vehicle once used by the detective.

Meanwhile, inside the speeding Cruiser 150 Vanessa with her foot on the gas pedal asks,

"Which of those sacks belongs to me or do I get what's inside the trunk?"

Levy and Coles stare at the three sacks of dough separating them on the rear seat.

"What's happening Cox, are you getting ready to jump ship?"

Coles questions.

Vanessa addresses:

"My mind is not there yet. I just want to know when this is all over what belongs to me. After all, I didn't sign up for all of this, I just wanted one of his little girls. I don't like being taken for granted. This is not police work. This is me. BTW, where is she? Where is Brianna?"

Her partners in crime both plead the fifth.

Vanessa continues,

"I underwent one accident with this car a year ago. The human side of me tells me that once is enough. You might say that we are all in this together, be strong and all that. That's not the point. I am strong. That's a given. However, we've been driving now for almost an hour since the robbery occurred, and no one has said: Vanessa this bag of money belongs to you, or you may have all that's in the trunk. Thanks for all your help in defending us against the enemies...Here is little Brianna.

This is not done, pro-bono gentlemen. I want to make sure that it is understood before we get in too deep."

"Yours is the one with the jewelry on top and the crisp bank notes straight from the vault. Seeing we have not had the time to determine what's in those sacks in the trunk, as soon as we get a chance to do, so we will split the sum three ways. Your wish will come true. Brianna is waiting for you as soon as we connect with the kidnappers."

Levy assures.

"Are these notes a legal tender? I am not sure that I can trust anything you say. You stayed so long in that bank I could have gotten busted. You said it would be a quick one. Next time you drive the getaway car, and you'll see how it feels."

Vanessa continues.

By this time, she feels as though things weren't done as the blueprint indicated. Levy got greedy once he saw the bags getting filled up with cash. He had no idea that the bank had so much money on hand. When he did, he wanted it all.

"They smell real, feel real and crisp, sound real, look real, but I didn't get a chance to taste them yet. And aren't you glad we cleaned house? BTW, thanks for taking out the two armored guys. We'll split evenly what's in the trunk."

Says Levy.

Vanessa states in a semi-jovial mode,

"Thanks for all you do. Not sure if I can say partners just yet. This is still a work in progress."

Levy and Coles look at each other not sure which one of them should address first. In Levy's way of thinking, he feels that Vanessa just wanted to vent her anger since their termination.

On the other hand, Coles feels that Vanessa is being broken down being the getaway driver. She apparently feels that if they should not have come out alive she would be satisfied that she gave them a piece of her mind.

Anyway, he informs,

"We are all in this together whether we live or die, so let's deal with solutions rather than the problems."

Says Levy,

"Come on let's be realistic. I trust no one, never."

Says Vanessa.

"He is right Vanessa... solutions."

Says Levy.

The Sherriff car proceeds speedily and is rapidly catching up with Cruiser 150.

BULLETS RING OUT LIKE popping corn on Pacific Coast Highway. Most of them scatter. A few rounds strike Cruiser 150 in the trunk area. The Sherriff cruiser, the CHP cruiser, and the red Mustang are all in pursuit of the getaway car. Cruiser 150 picks up velocity on the open road as other moving vehicles give way. The second round of bullets aimed at the rear windscreen from the Sherriff's car misses as Cruiser 150 changes lanes on this two-lane double highway, doing the max.

Robert Coles rolls down the window and gets a great aim at the Sherriff. He feels good about it. He shoots. That round of bullets shatters the windscreen and ricochets, hitting the Sherriff in the region of the neck. The Sherriff's car swerves off the road while the pursuing CHP cruiser clips its right rear fender. That impact:

1. Sends the Sherriff's car over the steep cliff.

2. Sends the CHP car into the gutter and up embankment rolling over several times back onto the open road.

3. Sends the pursuing Mustang into a 360 turn to avoid a collision into the side of the moving CHP cruiser.

The Mustang gains control on the road and is still in pursuit of the getaway car. Cruiser 150 takes a detour. Coles asks,

"What did Bob Marley say?"

"Could you be loved?"

Vanessa Cox answers.

"Wrong answer," replies Coles.

"Rat Race!"

Answers Levy.

"You blew it!

He said:

"I SHOT THE SHERIFF!"

Coles replies.

"You are right; Croft would have said unfriendly fire, Black on Black crime,"

Vanessa Cox interjects.

"The review board would have ruled it friendly fire. What a corrupt ... organization? A bunch of bureaucrats!"

Levy states.

In Bill Levy's mindset even if the BHPD offered him his job back, he would say:

"Go take a hike or better yet, take a long jump off a short plank."

Adding to that thought the loud noise of gunshots from above, plus the lowering shadow of an aircraft alerts them of the Police Chopper now in pursuit overhead.

Vanessa Cox asks,

"Which of you, guys ... would like to drive from here on?"

"This thing is so attached to you."

Says Levy,

"Not really,"

" Are you tired or something, Cox?"

Asks Levy.

"Vanessa you ought to be kidding... I thought to drive was your thing, and this machine was your baby ..."

Coles argues.

"No, I am not tired. We are inseparable, but I need a ... potty break."

Vanessa Cox insists, pleading her case.

Bullets continue to rain down from the overhead police helicopter patrol, and penetrating the Cruiser 150's roof.

"You should have seen the Bank Manager. His pants turned browner when I asked him to open the vault."

Levy states jokingly.

"Think fair weather without the gardening, Cox."

Says Coles,

"Guys, that's not helping the situation,"

Says Vanessa,

Vanessa speeds up as the helicopter continues its' vicious assault and pursuit. Coles and Levy respond with several rounds of their own.

The helicopter swoops down low in order to dismantle the cruiser and the three bank robbers. It descends lower than it should. The tunnel is now in close proximity.

Cruiser 150 speeds up and goes through the tunnel. It's way too late for the helicopter to regain altitude. As a result, it slams and crashes into the mountain above the tunnel, throwing debris and aircraft fragment wrapped up in a ball of fire onto the roadway.

Meanwhile, Detective Croft is still in pursuit on PCH. There is no Cruiser 150 in view. He steps on the pedal in order to catch up.

Croft radios in,

"Chopper, Chopper, come in. I've lost you. Are you out there?"

There's no response.

So he tunes into the radio.

The announcer continues,

"…Thank you for that comment. This is News Radio 88.7 FM. We are still following the multi-dimensional story which occurred in Beverly Hills on Christmas Eve. As far as we know the police-uniformed bank robbers who held up and robbed the First Nations Bank yesterday, are at the same time on the loose. Several motorists, two armored personnel, civilians, as well as police officers are left for dead. The death toll is now 10.

The robbers, believed to have been three ex-police officers made their getaway with a huge amount of cash and jewelry from the First Nations Bank, and a vast amount of cash from an Armored Truck. This undisclosed amount of cash and jewelry could be the largest combined heist in history.

Additionally, the nine-year daughter of detective John Croft - their ex-boss is still missing. It was reported that Brianna, age 9, was last seen escorted onto a bus at the Beverly Center by two men.

A reward of $30.000.00 will be awarded to anyone providing information leading up to their arrest."

John pounds his fist upon the dashboard several times. He contemplates, not knowing whether to continue or abort his pursuit. The news sinks in deeper like salt in the wound. How did his family get caught up in this fiasco? He questions.

Nevertheless, he continues in pursuit envisioning what he would do to the three scum bags when they are caught.

9

CROFT SEES A PAYPHONE at a rest stop. He pulls off the road and accesses it. He dials. Lieutenant Davis picks up. "Lieutenant Davis this is John Croft." Davis says.

"My apologies … detective Croft! I wished there was something we could have done to prevent this. We are doing all we can to bring them to justice and get your daughter back safely. No one has seen the alleged kidnappers or bus since it left the Beverly Center. Please understand that we are dealing with three veterans, officers who you yourself mentored."

"I feel like I am between a rock and a... hard place. Why is everyone so tight-lipped about Brianna's situation?"

Says John,

"I understand how you feel. If you are asking me for my opinion on what direction, you should take. That is totally your call. You have my support and that of the entire Beverly Hill Police Department. You must also understand we have to still address crime here in Beverly Hills. However, rest assured that we've got your back."

Davis reminds him.

"Where is the rest of my family? Who is handling their palladium 24/7?"

Asks John,

"They are at home. They are well protected by your fellow police officers."

Says Davis.

"Thanks, no more surprises"

Says John.

"How soon before you catch up with them, Croft?"

Asks Davis.

"I'm working on it."

John looks at the payphone in his hand and returns it to the hook with a slam. It's nightfall. He returns to the Mustang. He continues on that lonely stretch of the once scenic highway. He rolls down the car's window and breathes the salty Malibu oceanic air. He comes to a traffic signal which changes to red. He stops hoping for a sign of the getaway car. Suddenly, the Cruiser 150 makes a right turn at that same intersection heading west.

The bank robbers are oblivious of John's presence at the red light.

Cars are still waiting at the traffic light. Angry motorist's honk their horns in protest of Croft's going nowhere in traffic. He takes off and is now in close pursuit.

Up ahead on PCH steam emits from underneath the cruiser's hood.

Panic sets in on the part of the bank robbers.

"Guys we are in trouble,"

Vanessa states upon noticing the emission.

"It could be just a busted radiator hose. We are almost there."

Levy says.

"We are?"

Asks Vanessa.

The red Mustang is now in close view as Croft closes in on the Cruiser 150. John Croft gets a good aim to shoot through the rear windscreen and clipping both Levy and Coles.

Vanessa detects Croft's presence tailgating, through the rearview mirror and quickly skips lanes.

As a result, the round from Croft's gun misses everything but the bushes and the side street.

Croft notices steam evaporating from underneath the cruiser's hood and immediately sets up another aim at its' rear windscreen.

Meanwhile, Levy and Coles get an aim at the Mustang. Their shots are released. Both rounds connect with the Mustang's windscreen, shattering it and in the process knocking Croft's gun onto the rear seat and to fall onto the floor. Trying to recover it, he is unable to do so.

As a result, he loses control over the vehicle which zigzags across the median excessively. Not only, that, he is also gun-less. He composes himself as he tries keeping up with Cruiser 150.

Up ahead, the flow and the rate at which steam exudes from under the Cruiser's hood increases. The vehicle begins to reduce its speed due to considerable loss of power.

The road narrows and is now reduced to two-lane highway once again.

Up ahead bright lights welcome a flow of traffic heading in the opposite direction.

He removes his seat belt and takes the time to retrieve his gun. This time, he grabs it. He's elated as he gets ready to pick up a good aim on the Cruiser 150. His aim is on. He shoots. Two rounds from his gun remove its' rear windscreen as the bullets lodge in the vacant front passenger seat.

With the rear windscreen blown out, it is now obvious to him that his daughter isn't one of the passengers inside the Cruiser unless she's concealed inside the trunk.

Inside the Cruiser 150, it becomes uncomfortable for Vanessa as glass fragments reside between her and the driver's seat. Plus, the thickness of smoke from underneath the hood creates poor visibility for all.

Bill Levy, Robert Coles, and John are now in person for the first time since that meeting over a year ago.

This time, their lives are at stake as John's recovered gun is pointing at them while theirs are pointing at him. The one who shoots first wins as all of their aims are dead on. The Cruiser goes around the bend on the road.

The flow of traffic continues in the opposite direction. Suddenly, the bus approaches and merges for a slow head-on collision with the Cruiser 150.

Vanessa, quick and alert banks the Cruiser in the gutter.

As a result, the speeding Mustang crashes head-on with the bus. Croft gets thrown in the rear seat of the Mustang. He tries getting out but is unable to do so of his own accord.

Inside the Cruiser 150, the trio shakes them off.

"Let's go, guys, onto the bus. We've got to hurry."

Says Levy as he collects what's stashed in the trunk and depositing it inside a black trash bag.

The trio boards the bus, carrying their guns and multiple bags of cash.

10

ON THE BORDER OF BEVERLY HILLS and the city of Los Angeles, on Beverly Blvd and the corner of La Cienega Blvd nestles the Beverly Center. This shopping mall is the only one of its kind close to Beverly Hills' proximity located on La Cienega Blvd. Shoppers go on a bender at the mall. Events evolving from violence in Beverly Hills include the O.J. Simpson trial, otherwise known as the trial of the century. While neighboring, Los Angeles has experienced the Watts riots as well as the Rodney King police beatings. Police crimes have not only been a thing of the past but also of the present here in Southern California.

ABOUT ONE YEAR PRIOR to that major bank robbery at the Los Angeles/Beverly Hills border. A black automobile burning rubber as it U-turns on a partially crowded Melrose Street in Beverly Hills, California draws the attention of late evening pedestrians. A close-up of the vehicle, reveals a black SUV. This late model Chevy Tahoe sports limo style tinted windows. A flashing blue light illuminates and rotates briskly on its simonized dashboard.

The distorted transmission of a man's voice, via multiple 2-way radios captures the attention to the three police officers on board that vehicle for the second time. Then the sound comes in with much more vigor and clarity. The commanding transmitting male baritone voice echoes,

"175, South Doheny!"

It continues,

"The woods are lovely, dark and deep, but I've got promises to keep. And miles to go before I sleep."

The three officers inside the SUV clue in and the driver replies. The SUV speeds up, and like a fire engine in pursuit, it merges with traffic while other vehicles give way.

Moments later the vehicle pulls up and parks outside a dimly lit Beverly Hills mansion. The female driver, Vanessa Cox is a tall Caucasian in her mid to late 30s with a scar across her forehead. With a stern face, Vanessa investigates while she intently surveys her surroundings.

Vanessa hands over a ledger filled with names to one of her two male police associates, Robert Coles. Robert overlooks the document while he accommodates the Input of His Associate Bill Levy.

Bill is Hispanic of the same gender and leans forward while sitting on the rear seat in order to read. The trio nod in agreement.

Reminiscently, they heard that quote by Robert Frost used by their superior John Croft accompanying numerous dispatches. However, it now had a different cadence. Anyway, they wait, somewhat confused but poised, with a gun in hand while their double-parked vehicle idles.

On a weekend night, it is customary for many parked cars to occupy this crowded street, especially a few blocks away on Melrose Avenue. With the many restaurants, many executives are out having dinner.

Christmas carols - unplugged reverberates from inside the mansion as intoxicated attendees revel although in a festive mood.

Close-up on the living room table a mound of coke draws a crowd of attendees like flies to molasses. Adults and Young Adults alike assemble. Some partake while others observantly swagger, holding on to the filled to the brim and running over shot glasses in one hand and with a slice of lemon in their other hand. The mixed odor of liquor, marijuana, and multiple fragrances blends.

On that same street, a car pulls out from a parking space in front of the SUV. Wasting no time the SUV drives forward then reverses and parallel parks easily and nestles into that vacant parking spot. The passengers step out and head inside the mansion joining the other partygoers.

11

FURTHER UP THE STREET and almost out of view a black Mercedes Benz pulls up and waits. Inside, Detective John Croft sits with his ears to the ground.
A white supped up SUV approaching from the opposite direction of the Benz turns into the driveway in front of the surveillance parked SUV. A male Hispanic driver wearing an upscale white sweat suit,

accented by a baseball hat emerges. The Los Angeles Lakers basketball team logo makes him belong. The cap is turned backward and slightly twisted to the left. He gets out of the white vehicle and enters through the side door entrance of the Beverly Hills mansion.

The driver conducts business returns suddenly and re-boards his white SUV. He throws a small pouch inside the glove compartment, checks his side as well as rearview mirrors and then reverses his vehicle out of the driveway.

The three watchdog officers, Cox, Levy and Coles inside the black SUV acknowledge as the driver makes his undisturbed exit. They check his name on the list on the ledger. Then look each other in agreement. They know him. He's high priority circled in red.

The white vehicle heads north on Doheny Street in the direction of John Crofts' parked Mercedes Benz.

Detective Croft sitting, surveying, in that Mercedes, spots the oncoming SUV. He gets out of his car and signals a pull over to the curb.

The driver accommodates. Croft embarks on a routine check on the driver.

"Where are you coming from and where are you going?"

The man stutters his answer,
"From home and going to work…"
"Where do you work?"
The detective asks.
"Key Club on Sunset,"
Replies the driver.
"Your drivers' license and proof of insurance sir,"
States detective Croft.
The driver asks.
"I wasn't speeding … what is the matter …?"
"Just a simple … routine check! Sit tight."
Replies detective Croft.
The driver is hesitant concerning handing over the requested documents. Croft realizes that the driver is high in the list of narcotics pushers according to the profile on his most-wanted list.
"Step out of the vehicle!"
Croft Says.
The driver hesitatingly accommodates.
"Up against the… vehicle! With your hands on the top of your head!"
He complies.
Croft frisks him.
He is clean.
Croft handcuffs the wanted man who now crouches and sits at the roadside.

Croft continues the search of the vehicle and opens the glove compartment. There he recovers the black pouch. Croft opens it. Inside he discovers about one-sixteenth of a kilo of cocaine neatly packaged. He re-seals the package.

Walking over to his car Croft throws the package of narcotics on the front seat. He grabs the driver and forces him in the rear seat of his Mercedes-Benz.

Croft uses his cellular and calls for a tow and backup. He waits for them to show up.

The tow truck tows away the white SUV.

Meanwhile, a dispatched police cruiser arrives, racing to the scene. Croft pulls the man out of the black Benz and forces him inside the cruiser. The cruiser drives off.

The three surveillance police officers in the Tahoe are oblivious about these recent events orchestrated by their boss John Croft around the bend and up the street out of their view. It's time to break the seal on that bottle of Grey Goose Vodka underneath the front passenger seat. Vanessa does. She pours into three plastic glasses. They cheer, down their drinks and share a pack of chewing gum.

A red Mustang pulls up into the driveway of the mansion from the same direction as did the white SUV. Robert Coles steps out and conducts a make belief ID check on the African American driver. He gives the driver the green light as he emerges into the drug spot. The driver ambles inside through the front door and saunters towards the back room. He makes his drug purchase.

Meanwhile, the shades over the window panes retract as partygoers get their view of the SUV with the three uniformed officers inside.

Inside the mansion the partygoers yell,

"Cops! Pigs! Undercover!"

Some dash for cover. While the really toasted ones act as if they don't care.

The host, a man in his 30s comes to the window. He looks through the shades and replies.

"They know me. It's all good! Those are my Niggers. Don't worry about a thing. Let's party hardy."

The party continues uninterrupted as it escalates. Even the music gets turned up much louder.

A woman wearing the tightly fitted pair of blue jeans as if stitched to her body brings in a plate of meatballs and toothpicks on a plate in one hand. In the other hand, she carries another plate, along with a zip-lock bag and a large table spoon. Some seemed to be starving attendees reach for a toothpick. They fetch meatballs others eye the other plate intensely.

With these wares, the woman in the sexy jeans creates a fresh mound of coke on the center table. You should see the big smiles on the faces of the salivating drug users. Some dealing with their leftovers from the previous serving take the time to add to their already existing "line" of the substance before indulging.

In the interim, back on the street, the driver of the Mustang makes his departure out of the driveway and heads in the opposite direction away from Detective Croft's hideout.

Meanwhile, inside the Tahoe, the three police officers enjoy Grey Goose Vodka now mixed with eggnog in a festive mood. They are having such a jolly good time, one worth remembering.

The Christmas lights hanging from the mansion sway back and forth casting their glowing reflection on the vehicles parked on South Doheny Street. While the wind whistles through the trees and the leaves applause.

The partying on the inside continues as another plate of cocaine is brought into the living room from sales room. The partygoers dive in aggressively and snort all the substance.

12

ANOTHER CALL COMES INTO the three officers transmitted over the same static filled police radio. Once again, it's that interchangeable voice, that of Detective Croft, except at this time he sounds a bit more sarcastic.

"The woods are lovely, dark and deep, but I've got promises to keep. And miles to go before I sleep."

Croft continues,

"What is your 20?"

"175 South Doheny,"

Replies Robert Coles.

How is the surveillance going? Is there anything to report?

Asks Detective Croft.

Coles replies,

"Ten - four, boss! Nothing to report! A white SUV showed up. The driver a Hispanic male dropped off a wrapped present to the host. Then he left. Other partygoers seem to be having a good time. There isn't anything really unusual happening. Just Christmas Carols, not even some Tupac Shakir Rap music or Notorious Big's."

After that fabricated report by Robert Coles, Bill Levy replies from the rear seat in the black Chevy Tahoe:

"Not much of anything on this block, sir."

"Quiet night so far, huh? ... "

Replies Detective Croft,

"That's all she wrote," interrupts Vanessa Cox.

Robert Coles nods in total agreement.

Croft looks at his Rolex watch, personalizing it while he gets the time. He develops a thought and then rushes to the trunk of his car where he retrieves a red and white Santa Claus hat. Like a kid, he treats it like his first beanie. He affixes it to his head covering most of his face and begins to hum, *Rudolph the Red Nose Reindeer*. Now semi-masked Detective Croft takes the wheel and drives off in a jolly mood towards to the Beverly Hills mansion.

Moments later, Croft pulls up past the Tahoe and enters the driveway.

The three officers inside the Tahoe Levy, Coles, and Vanessa Cox ignore who in their mind is a possible new narcotics client. They are totally unaware that it's their boss detective Croft who just drove up into the driveway. His disguise is superb. They are a bit toasted.

Croft enters the mansion from the side entrance of the house. The music is more than Christmas music. Metal Rock and a mixture of House Music blasts as he enters through that side door and inside the drug spot. Anyway, he focuses on his objective.

Inside the room: the vibe is cozy, semi-lit with a large empty black leather couch. Not at all a good match for the - brown wall interior decoration. It doesn't matter to Detective John Croft if there is a hidden camera or not, he acts the part of the buyer and is playing it well. He is not only in his element but comfortable with his new under-cover-look. He smiles, feeling totally in control over the situation.

Croft sees a closed door. He knocks on it. There's no response. Suddenly, a lid opens up in the middle of the door.

"How much?"

The raspy female voice asks.

"Two-sixteenth,"

Replies Croft in that baritone voice,

He puts the money through the slot.

The seller counts it and pushes the package through the slot.

"You need any meth? There's a discount when you purchase two-sixteenths…?"

She asks,

"Not today, I'm good."

Says detective Croft.

Croft takes receipt of the drugs and makes his exit through the side door. He gets inside his car and drives away.

The officers inside the Tahoe pay not much of any attention to Croft as he exits the driveway either. They are wrapped up in cutting up among themselves conversationally. At this point, they are no longer sober. They are intoxicated from all that Grey Goose Vodka as the bottle is now empty. Vanessa tries desperately to keep a level head. Unable, Vanessa acts and replies over the top. Her companions present her with one-dollar bills for her performance. She giddily accepts.

CROFT IS NOW OUT of their sight as he hits the street. He puts the two packages of narcotics inside a plastic bag. He removes his red and white hat and places it on the passenger seat next to him. He starts up his car, checks the sides and rearview mirror and then drives back on Burton Way to the Beverly Hills Police Station.

13

UNKNOWN, TO OFFICERS Vanessa Cox, Bill Levy, and Robert Coles, Detective Croft their boss returned to 175 South Doheny later that night along with two other officers to comb through the scene. Upon arrival, they arrested the owner of the mansion along with the host at the party 32-year-old Emanuel Friar. Both men were charged with selling illegal drugs and running a narcotics spot.

No one, not even the desk Sergeant was allowed to talk about that arrest to anyone over the weekend. It was not publicized. Luckily, for the precinct, it was kept confidential. Coles, Levy, and Cox were already scheduled to have that weekend off.

IT'S MONDAY MORNING and its business as usual at the Beverly Hills Police Station. Croft though is on a mission. He sits in the head seat of the large table in the small conference room. Vanessa Cox, Bill Levy, and Robert Coles face Detective Croft in a semi-circle. This is a rather unusual beginning of the week meeting for the trio, though they have been there before but on two separate Friday afternoons for turning in a small quota of citations, Halloween night and New Year's Eve.

Anyway, they brace themselves unaware as to how this situation will all play out.

Croft addresses the trio sarcastically,

"So how was your Saturday night rendezvous?"

Vanessa Cox replies,

"Rendezvous?"

Croft interjects,

"Well, there were no citations issued, no arrests made. In my opinion, it seemed like it was an off-night for you three. An ordinary civilian would have made at least one arrest. This is not the first time you have not reached your quota. This time, all three bins bearing your names are empty."

"There was no one to arrest. How could you arrest someone if they haven't committed a crime?"

Asks Vanessa Cox bluntly.

Bill Levy in support,

"Boss, you know Beverly Hills as much as we do. People are afraid to drive a bad car in that neighborhood. They fear they will get pulled over. If demographically they don't fit in, they stay on the Sunset Strip until they get to Hollywood. The Strip is as far as they come west. Others pick up Sunset Boulevard heading west after the 405 Freeway and on into the Pacific Palisades. The prestige is too much for them. Plus they would expect the residents to police themselves, knowing that every homeowner apparently owns at least one handgun and two automobiles.

We were dispatched to 175 Doheny, to monitor a Christmas party. Attendees were just singing and listening to a bunch of Christmas carols. It was a quiet night. You were the one who made that call."

Robert Coles interjects,

"The most likely traffic violation is a motorist running that red light at Santa Monica Boulevard and Sunset or a high profile domestic dispute. Something more severe than that is highly unlikely for that neighborhood. Plus, it's Christmas."

Croft's boss, Lieutenant Davis, a slender built Caucasian in his mid-fifties, sporting a well-manicured mustache walks in and pulls up a chair next to Croft.

Three pairs of eyes are now focused on the two superiors at the top of that table.

"I don't buy any of that bull. There are many reasons why a police station is in this city. If I sent my daughters on the beat, they would have identified criminals."

Croft lifts a small duffel bag off the floor, unzips it. He pulls out an empty Grey Goose Vodka bottle and places it on the table in front of Coles, Levy, and Cox. The trio is now poker-faced as they listen to the charges as well as seeing the evidence presented against them.

Croft addresses,

"In order to convict anyone there has to be substantial evidence, wouldn't you agree?"

Levy replies,

"Right."

Vanessa Cox, staring at the bottle,

"Well that depends on,"

"On what, Vanessa Cox?"

Asks Lieutenant Davis.

"The extenuating circumstances,"

Interjects Coles.

"How extenuating is drinking on the job and being so drunk you forget to discard of the empty bottle? Pretty circumstantial."

Asks Croft.

Officer Vanessa Cox still pleads the fifth.

Lieutenant Davis following up Croft addresses,

"In 2006, around 20,000 people died in the U.S. in alcohol-related traffic crashes...In 2009, about four people were killed in alcohol-impaired driving fatalities for every 100,000 Americans."

Levy as if answering for his colleagues, replies,

"We all know the stats' Lieutenant."

Vanessa Cox and Robert Coles concur with a nod of their head.

Croft reaches for the duffel bag and pulls out a stack of photographs.

He lays a picture of a Hispanic man wearing a Laker's cap and in handcuffs on the table.

"Was this man Caesar Escobar at 175 S. Doheny that night?"

Levy upset, yells,

"Many people were at that Christmas Party. Is this some type of interrogation tactic?"

Lieutenant Davis replies,

"Answer the question. What's the crucible?"

The three officers are mute. No one dares to confess.

Croft throws the pouch on the table which he confiscated from Caesar, along with pictures of the White SUV hoisted on the tow truck. Next, he reaches inside his small pouch and pulls out his packet of narcotics.

"This is my stash of narcotics, I purchased that night at 175 S. Doheny, while the premises were surveyed by three of Beverly Hills' finest: Officers Robert Coles, Bill Levy and Vanessa Cox. Methamphetamine was offered also, but I declined."

Croft unfolds the package revealing the two-sixteenth kilo of white uncut cocaine.

Looking at the overwhelming evidence on the table, Lieutenant Davis states,

"There has to be some kind of explanation of the type of behavior."

"I need my lawyer,"

Replies Cox.

"I plead the fifth,"

Says Levy.

"This is bad police business! The worse ..."

Yells Robert Coles.

This … stinks,

Says Vanessa Cox.

"It a stinker. Later, that night two of your fellow officers accompanied me back to 175 Doheny. There we arrested the homeowner along with the party's host. They were booked that same night and face charges of operating a drug spot and the selling of illegal drugs."

The three officers are stunned.

John continues,

"So to encapsulate, I made three arrests on three nights ago at the same location where you failed to make one."

Detective Croft states:

Davis gives Croft a confident look.

"I must inform you officers. On that block, we've installed security cameras." Says Davis as he opens his bag and places the tape footage on the table. "That night's activities are on film." Croft gives Davis a surprised look.

"Officers my hands are tied I have no choice but to issue a six-month suspension pending a review board hearing."

Vanessa Cox replies.

"I quit! To heck with the review board…"

Vanessa opens her purse and throws her badge on the table. It ricochets off the Grey Goose bottle.

Bill Levy explodes,

This is B.S. to the highest…

Robert Coles interrupts.

"This is bad police business. Once a Con Man, always a Con Man. I have miles to go before I sleep, yep! I know. My miles are up!"

Coles and Levy toss their badge onto the table. They accidentally connect with the vodka bottle. The trio stormed out of the room, leaving Croft and Davis to clean up the evidence.

14

INSIDE THE WRECKED BUS ON PCH. Brianna, Detective Croft's daughter is awake but still dazed, tied up and blindfolded. The tape is bandaged around her mouth. The two kidnappers accommodate the newly arrived passengers. Without wasting any time, Bill Levy takes the wheel. After all, he has the blueprint. The driver accommodates.

Levy says,

"We are heading for the ship. Great job guys, perfect timing, we are only a few miles away. However, we've got to hurry."

Robert Coles looks across at Vanessa.

"You rock VC! Superb driving skills!"

He comments,

Vanessa replies with,

"Ditto!"

Vanessa is indeed flattered but acknowledges with a smile underneath her comment. Meanwhile, the kidnapped Brianna captures her attention. Brianna reflects on spending time with her two sisters, waiting for them at the entrance into her classroom as they arrive to pick her up and board the school bus which takes them home. Even though its Christmas break, her missing her sisters takes her back to that particular golden moment. She tears up in the moment.

Vanessa begins to comfort the nine-year-old, first by checking her neck for her temperature along with her other vital signs.

The bus journeys on. It exits off PCH and onto Beach Street. Nestled in between some trees this narrow street empties out onto the beach. Black unlit coals leave their residue along with ash close to several barbecue pits. While empty beer bottles add to the untidiness of beachgoers who failed to clean up after themselves.

At sea, the ship, a roll-on-roll-off used for transporting vehicles waits. The sailor busily conducts his quick surveillance.

The bus driver drives the vehicle straight onto the ship.

The sailor immediately starts the ships' engine. The white water stirred up behind it indicates its readiness to depart.

Levy notices the tire impressions on the beach and orders the two kidnappers to get on it.

"There's a broom, erase our tracks! Hurry or we sail without you."

The two men race along the beach. They sweep the sand back together where the buses tire marks were etched. They scurry back onto the ship.

The ship already in motion lifts anchor and sails.

Levy and Coles remove the cash and stores securely in the ships' cabin. The trio shed their police attire and emerges on deck, wearing white sailor outfits.

Cox escorts Brianna into the hull of the ship. She removes the gag from Brianna's mouth and gives her a bottle of water. Brianna guzzles it down. After which she utters her first words after being kidnapped.

"What's going on?
Where are my parents?
Why am I tied up and with strangers?"
Brianna questions in frustration.
"We are going to the Caribbean. We might even see the Titanic. You never know."
Replies Vanessa.
"How can I see the Titanic if I can't see you?
One, I am hungry.
Two, very upset.
Three, where is my Barbie?
Four, Where are my parents?
Five, I don't even know your names. Very confusing for a nine-year-old, don't you think?"
States Brianna.
Vanessa goes to the galley and returns with fruits on a platter.
She observes as Brianna ravenously devours three whole bananas.
"Barbie will be there when we arrive. When you are finished eating, be sure to get some sleep, you look very tired, Brianna."
Vanessa concludes.

IN THE MEANTIME, back at the scene of Detective John Croft's accident an ambulance pulls up accompanied by a fire engine and police escorts. They cut away the front passenger door and removes Croft from the wreckage. They place him on a gurney. Paramedics attend to Croft. He remains in a coma. His only vital sign is a pulse. A helicopter touches down and airlifts Croft to the hospital.

Two tow trucks arrive and remove the Cruiser 150 and the Mustang. While CHP Officers collect evidence from the scene. Circling police helicopters fail to clue in on the getaway scene at sea.

15

BACK AT THE BEVERLY HILLS Police station officers discovered that the fingerprints lifted from inside the bank and on the two armored men matched those of Robert Coles and Bill Levy. Officers gait from place to place inside the station. They weigh the supporting evidence regarding those three officers involuntarily incorporated within their daily tasks.

It was quite obvious in their minds that now these bank-robbing ex-officers had made their getaway.

Many innocent people are left dead at the scene of the robbery. While three bank robbers pulled off one of the biggest heists ever in history.

The news about this crime was creating some repercussions to be faced by the shattered BHPD.

Detective Croft's nine-year-old daughter was not only kidnapped but not heard from since Christmas Eve. No one had even claimed responsibility for her kidnapping.

As the day waned, Detective Croft recently banged up in that almost fatal accident was now wheeled into the ER from the helicopter's landing pad.

Officers facilitating outside the ER certainly had a lot to chew on.

The news continued to spread, and many criminals and criminal minded individuals disclosed: "It takes police officers to pull off a crime like this one." Pick up a paper and you'll see it in print. At the barber shops, green rooms, parks, transit system, everywhere people were forming their own opinions regarding the robberies and kidnapping. How did three ex-police officers rob a bank so close to Beverly Hills, and an armored truck in succession? Then took off with all that money along with orchestrating the kidnapping of their ex-boss' nine-year-old daughter and made such an orchestrated getaway? Some gossipers bluntly stated; "This is not only a wake-up call for the BHPD but that police officer who are terminated from their jobs should be monitored for a period of time after their dismissal from *power*."

As the news continued to unfold, it was discovered that many of the high-end stores on the ritzy Rodeo Drive were the clients of First Nations Bank. Many had made their deposits the night before and some their deposits on that same day before the robbery occurred. The armored truck showed up to collect all of that dough. It was determined, however, if the robbery was pulled off an hour and a half later, the armored truck which was half full, would have picked up a great portion of the cash stolen from that Bank.

Police at BHPD were looking for answers. They realized, though, that it would have been a lot easier to solve civilian on civilian crime rather than law enforcement officers carried out offenses; most law enforcement officers know the short cuts and tricks to the trade. This was making their investigation more complicated.

Meanwhile, Lieutenant Davis comes under strong criticism from many Focus GROUPS. They claimed if the department had let the investigative board handle the disciplinary procedures involving the police officers. Things could have been swept under the rug. Beverly Hills, at this time, is swarmed with police vehicles on just about every street corner as officers stake out looking for any evidence of the crime. They now questioned how much, or is there any of their American freedom left?

While many wished the robbers get caught, others didn't give a darn, feeling it was a way to beat the system – stealing from those who have it. The beefed-up police presence in Beverly Hills continued for many days. If you looked like a criminal, smelled like a criminal, talked like a criminal, drove like a criminal, or you are a criminal rest assured you will be questioned as if you were in some way connected to that crime. So as a result, many avoided the police. Talk show after talk show, news report after news report took the time to vomit on the situation in one way or the other. The word on the street was; in addition to the gossip regarding the crime; if you don't like what's happening with the BHPD, write to your councilman and be aware of bad cops.

Meanwhile, the man feeling it most was Lieutenant Davis. Had it not been his decision to have Detective John Croft spy on those three officers, things might not have gone this way - like sour milk at the BHPD. But he was also spying on everyone including John.

16

THE GETAWAY SHIP embraces and battles the treacherous waves of the Pacific Ocean, heading south -south easterly towards Mexico. Levy calls Brian Mendez a Mexican Donald Trump type real estate investor and developer to get his 20 and an ETA into Mexico. Brian arranged to meet Levy at sea in order to arrange for the setting up of multiple businesses in Bermuda. The stage had already been set.   Brian Mendez informed Levy by text that he would be flying in from Los Angeles and would meet the ship in Mexico's harbor.

Levy met in privacy on the ship with Mendez. Brian, a real estate tycoon worked extensively in the Caribbean. He was known as the man responsible for the setting up of many hotels, restaurants along with other businesses. Brian worked with many drug dealers as well as racketeering gurus in his 5-year career. They provided the money, and he negotiated with the land owners and the builders, paid them and walked away from the deal after handing over the property to the investor. Brian never worked with banks and other financial institutions; it had to be cash, to avoid any paper trail. In a world filled with mistrust, he got paid in full every time. He gave the investors his word, and then he always delivered.

As the middle man, Brian Mendez stayed away from ownership. His investors loved him in the islands because after taking their money, he always delivered.

The getaway ship docked in Mexico and Brian was brought on board. After meeting with Levy, plans were set for building two hotels in Bermuda, a familiar territory to Mendez.

Mendez got paid his consulting fee from the loot by Levy, and the balance was due after the builders were given the go ahead. Levy then shook hands with Mendez. The developer picked up his briefcase now loaded with crisp twenty and fifty-dollar bills. As he began to walk away Levy shot him in the back with the aid of a silencer on his gun. Levy retrieved his money and then threw Mendez's body overboard with an iron sinker attached. He then hosed down the bloody remains.

Levy felt that he had gotten the information he needed and no longer needed Brian Mendez. He now knew the names of the people in Bermuda who built the properties and delivered. Plus he had the money to pay them.

Levy later rejoins Coles, who was not invited up.

"How was your meeting?"

Asks Coles,

"It went great; I can't wait to arrive in Bermuda."

States Bill Levy.

"Not going to let me in on it?"

Asks Coles.

"First, I need to see if it's all it's cut out to be."

Says Levy,

"You know I'm an opportunist,"

Says Coles.

"Yep."

Levy then confirms with the captain regarding the ETA in Bermuda. Coles, although not in on the hotels deal with Levy; he wasn't invited despite his entrepreneur's mindset. No one was. Even so, Coles was anxious to arrive on the island of Bermuda. The captain reassures the ETA.

Meanwhile, Vanessa locks the door of the hull, with the tied-up Briana. She takes the keys and heads to the deck.

In the interim, Brianna manages to untie herself and looks for an escape route. She wonders and finds none. So she stares at the porthole with teary eyes.

ON DECK, the Sea Captain who spits out residue from the chewed up tobacco in his mouth at intervals says.

"It could take us at least a month to arrive in Bermuda, that's if we go through the Panama Canal. We could hit the Panama Canal in less than one week."

Vanessa stares at both Levy and Coles pondering that statement. In her mind, she was expecting an earlier arrival time. The stop in Mexico in her mind had absolutely nothing to do with her, just with a becoming selfish Bill Levy, who did not include this in the plans prior to pulling off the planned heist.

INSIDE THE HULL, Brianna after feeling trapped within the world where she doesn't belong re-ties herself the best she could. How she wishes she could not only be with her sisters but talk to mom about the events she has undergone. Brianna wishes she could hear those bedtime stories her dad used to tell on those few nights when he was at home. Of course, she is completely unaware that her dad was involved in an almost fatal accident and is still hospitalized at this point. The homesick blues have gotten to her, so she finds herself a corner in the room where she sits and cries some more.

17

MEANWHILE, AT THE Los Angeles hospital Detective John Croft finally snaps out of the coma. He now has his sense of awareness back except that he could not remember how he got to be lying on a hospital bed. He looks up and recognizes his wife Elizabeth at his bedside. At first, the prognosis was bleak. There was a strong possibility; they may have had to amputate the leg because his blood failed to clot. However, during his sleep, the leg began to heal.

In the interim, news broke about a bus which washed ashore on Yuma Beach in Malibu. Moments later, police swarm the scene, including the traffic police who was last seen directing traffic at the Beverly Center where Brianna was kidnapped. The officer identified the bus as the one which left the scene where the nine-year-old was taken, hostage.

Police searched the bus thoroughly but found no evidence to link the bus to the crime, not even a single fingerprint. The only thing they had to go on was the word of the traffic police officer. There was no evidence to link the suspects, Coles, Levy or Cox.

Croft sitting up in bed watches the news and can't believe what has transpired as there seems to be no trace of foul play involving the washed ashore bus. To him, his daughter's disappearance now seems like an Alfred Hitchcock mystery.

PRIOR TO THE BUS SHOWING up at Yuma Beach, the Captain, his crew and Coles, Levy and Cox discussed what they should do with the bus now aboard the ship.

Here is how it all went down.

The Captain, chewing on tobacco asks,

"If we happen to get checked by coast guards or while in port in Mexico, this bus could alert them to an entire search of this ship."

The captain informs.

Levy thinks hard and then suggests,

"What if we were to dump it at sea as we go?"

Vanessa, locking in on the bus and on Levy thinks she hears Mexico. Simultaneously, she replies.

"Dump this? You've got to be kidding me.

She continues,

Why Mexico…?"

"We will make a service stop. Plus I need to renew an acquaintance while the ship is being serviced. The bus that's a possibility but we are going to have to do it at night, and away from these Malibu waters."

Says Bill Levy,

"Why so?"

Asked Vanessa,

"Just in case it should float back to the Malibu shore, they could follow our tracks thus, making going to the Caribbean a buried idea. In moments, we could be swarmed by Coasts Guards."

Says Bill Levy,

Vanessa, nodding her head finally concurs.

Then as if awaking from a nightmarish sleep, Vanessa utters:

"That's right the evidence. Fingerprints…! Lifting them could be a difficult process."

"Right,"

Says Levy,

Levy and Coles depart briskly to the hull of the ship. They, as swiftly as they departed, return to the deck, and board the bus wearing white wool gloves. The ex-police officers embark upon searching for any evidence containing DNA such as blood, hair, body fluids and or fingerprints with the aid of a magnifying glass.

Vanessa joins them in the evidence removal effort with rubber gloves and a bucket. She pours in Clorox, and a bottle of Vodka, short of a shot glass amount. Holding the Grey Goose bottle to her head, she downs it.

The two kidnappers who operated the bus observe as Vanessa Cox wearing a pair of rubber gloves mixes the ingredients in a bucket.

With the aid of baby wipes which Vanessa retrieves from the buses' first-aid kit, she proceeds to remove the fingerprints evidence from the bus.

The other two ex-police officers oversee the print's removal process. They then assist by dusting baby powder retrieved from the same kit over the once affected areas.

Coles and Levy then consult with the Captain. Both ex-policemen walk over to the bus. Levy gets in and starts up the engine. The captain clears the path. He returns to the helm. The ship speeds up.

Meanwhile, Levy puts the bus in reverse, releases the parking brake, and jumps out to safety. The bus speeds off the roll-on-roll-off and plunges into the deep. The turbulence and waves created by its departure rock the boat viciously from side to side and bow to be stern.

Inside of the hull, Brianna gets tossed up against the porthole and admiringly sees the bus submerge. She looks over at Vanessa with concern while trying to maintain her balance.

Vanessa seems occupied and self-centered.

Brianna asks,

"How are we getting off of this ship? Are we going to have to swim ashore and get attacked by the big fish, Jaws III?"

Vanessa says to Briana, as she turns out the light to crescendo leaving her in a lock down.

"No, we don't. You watch too many movies, little girls, go to bed!"

18

ONE MONTH LATER bad weather ensues near the Bermuda Triangle. The blast of thunder reverberates against the ship. The crack of lightning seems to open up a streak of light amidst the dark clouds across the night sky. The ship rocks back and forth; as it gets tossed around by the high seas and treacherous winds. The ship eventually splits its' mast. Water flows inside in barrel size portions.

The entire crew except for the captain of the helm is busily engaged in emptying the ship of its deluge. The sacks of money belonging to Coles, Levy and Cox are beginning to get soaked. Panic sets in on their part watching trouble at sea unfold.

Meanwhile, inside the hull, Brianna holds on to the bed head for her dear life, as the ship rocks continuously.

Levy frantically locates a box containing a roll of large black plastic trash bags. He distributes a few to Coles and Cox. They immediately insulate their bags of money from the fresh water downpour as well as the salt water combatant.

The flustered captain spits out tobacco residue and announces:

"We are going to have to abandon this ship! There's a slim chance of it making its way to shore safely. It is water logged and going down as a result of the weight caused by the gallons of water it has collected from both rain and sea.

Although the Bermuda shoreline seems to be only a few miles away, the intensity of the wind and waves leaves a slim chance of the ship arriving safely."

Bill Levy approaches the captain pointing his gun in his face.

"I hear what you say, but I have always believed in possibilities. You are going to have to get us ashore safely. Figure out a way! I paid you to get us there safely."

Says Levy as he and Coles continue their con-flotation of the captain.

Meanwhile, in the hull, Vanessa and Brianna are in a heated discussion.

Brianna repeats herself,

"I saw all this coming. You all are evil, and that's why the wrath of God has come upon you."

Vanessa slaps Brianna.

"We are going to be okay. We will weather the storm and get to shore safely. We have this very much under control."

Brianna in tears says,

"That's not what I heard. The captain just said that we may have to abandon ship All the money in those sacks cannot change the outcome. The love of money is the root of it all. You can't hide from God. I want to be with my family. Not with a bunch of thieves, robbers, and evil con-artists. I saw that man get killed in Mexico."

'What man? No man got killed in Mexico."

Answers Vanessa,

"Alright, whatever."

Vanessa slaps Brianna hard in the face with her right hand. Brianna feels it and tears up some more.

Suddenly, a huge wave rocks the ship almost causing it to submerge.

Coles and Levy stare questioningly at Brianna, and Vanessa caught up in a heated debate. Brianna sheds tears, once more.

The Captain announces,

"We are going to have to abandon ship. Everyone will be required to wear a life vest. This is for your own safety. Feel free to take your personal belongings with you, but I would recommend that you leave them behind. If the ship somehow makes it to shore after we disembark it will be easier to recover them than to risk lives trying to save them now."

Brianna not only dries the tears from her eyes but retrieves her rough draft of a Barbie doll from under the pillow. She clutches onto the sketch of Barbie for dear life.

On the other hand, Vanessa stares at her two sacks of loot in wonderment as to how it will all go down leaving her without any money.

Vanessa, as if what the Captain said just finally sank in.

"What did he say? That is bullshit!"

Levy says to Coles,

"I am taking over this ship!"

Levy enters the room. The Captain reaches for his gun and aims it at Levy. Showing superior gun skills, Levy draws his gun and caps the captain. The Captain falls dead to the floor. Levy throws him overboard in the same fashion, he eliminated Brian Mendez. Brianna hides her face as she reminisces on the Mexican tragedy. Levy grabs control at the helm of the ship. Coles gets ready to wash the blood off the ship with the water hose. A wave surges almost covering the ship. That flow of water washes the blood off the ship and into the ocean.

Weather conditions worsen instead of getting better. Instead of heading for the shore the ship begins to drift speedily towards the deep. Not only, that, the sailor's assistant who has been laboring continuously to rid the ship of the water intake is also missing. No one seems to know his whereabouts. They, however, assume the man jumped ship.

Coles is the only option for bailing out the water as Vanessa is still busy with the getting acquainted with each other dilemma, with Brianna.

The ship continues to drift out of control.

Vanessa assembles her two sacks. One strapped across her back by a rope, the other over her left arm. She plunges into the deep holding onto Brianna with the other hand. Brianna holds on tightly to her drawing of Barbie.

Amidst the treacherous waves, Vanessa kicks desperately with her feet.

Brianna paddles with both of her hands and feet towards the shore.

Coles and Levy quickly grab their sacks and plunge into the deep. A huge wave finally takes the ship under.

19

BACK AT THE HOSPITAL, detective John Croft hobbles around on his injured leg, still inside the cast. He reaches for the Los Angeles Times newspaper on top of the dresser. In the meantime, his cell phone rings. He fumblingly retrieves the phone from his pocket and answers it on the fourth ring. The newspaper now becomes an abandoned thought.

Could this be the great news, he is longing to hear regarding his kidnapped daughter Brianna?

"Hello, this is John Croft"

He says.

"Hey honey, it's Liz. How are you feeling today?"

Asks his wife Elizabeth,

"Great! Getting in shape,"

Says Croft.

"Any news as yet on Brie, John? I am really worried that she will never return to us alive. It has been several weeks now."

Continues Elizabeth.

"Nothing yet, except that Lieutenant Davis called earlier and informed me that the bus was towed to the pound and searched a second time for evidence; in addition to being scrutinized by the crime lab. But the detectives came up empty,"

Answers Croft, who continues:

"On the upside, the doctor says that I could remove the cast next week. Then after two weeks of rehab, my leg should be as good as before. I will have to take this on myself. Probably return to jogging every morning."

"That is great news!"

Says Elizabeth.

"Yep! This is a mission only one man can fill. How are the kids?"

Replies John Croft.

"They miss you at home, John. I told them that you would be home soon. They still think that it is your fault why Brianna is missing. Now they are even blaming me for shopping too much that day in the mall."

Replies Elizabeth.

"Elizabeth let me talk to them,"

Croft says.

"Okay. Hold on."

Elizabeth rounds up the kids who are upstairs playing hide and seek.

"Your DAD is on the phone."

Paula, the eldest picks up the phone.

"Hello, Dad!"

"Hello, how are you sweet pea?"

"Sad!"

Paula replies.

"Why are you sad?"

Croft asks.

"Because you are not at home, and neither is Brie."

"Cheer up, Daddy will be home next week, and he is going to find Brianna wherever she is."

"Whatever!' They said that Brie had been eaten up by a big bad shark."

"Who told you that?"

"That's what most of the kids in school were saying today. Don't lie to me Daddy. Is she or isn't she already dead … eaten up by Jaws?"

"We don't know for sure, but I will be going in search of your little sister when I get out of the hospital. And when I find her I will bring her kidnappers to justice."

"And when is that Daddy?"

The doctor says next week. I believe him, it could be sooner."

"I thought you told us to love others but trust no one. The doctor could be lying."

"He is not. Where is Denise?"

Croft asks,

She refuses to come to the phone, John. She is in the bedroom crying."

Says Elizabeth,

The waiting nurse signals to Detective Croft that it is time to check his temperature.

Croft looks at the cell phone now removed from his ear and lying flat in his hand. He returns the phone to his ear.

"I've got to go. Tell mom to call me later. Daddy will be home soon. I will find your baby sister."

The nurse draws the curtain and takes John's temperature and blood pressure. She remakes the bed and gathers up the used drinking glass.

Detective Croft turning to her asks,

"Is everything okay?"

The nurse remarks,

"Mr. Croft you need to relax a bit. Your blood pressure is 125 over 80. You are also running a fever."

She places her instruments on the tray and walks out of the room carrying the tray and the used utensil.

20

IN BERMUDA, VANESSA COX, Bill Levy, Robert Coles and Brianna finally make it ashore safely, amidst the pouring rain. Vanessa carries Brianna on her back while toting her bag of cash and jewelry in one hand. Coles and Levy carry theirs on their backs. They notice a rundown shed, in the distance, along the beach and move into that direction to avoid the pouring rain. The shed is vacant with a few half-empty beer bottles, sea shells, gravel and sea sand.

Next to the shed is an old parked Volkswagen Beetle. Levy darts towards the jalopy and tries jump-starting the vehicle for several minutes to no avail. Then he tries to roll starting it while Coles pushes it down the slope. The car is non-responsive. Both men return to the shed and rest after a while. Brianna is trembling as a result of being exposed to too much wetness within the last twenty-four hours.

Moments later, the rain tapers off so they continue on foot along the beach with Vanessa carrying Brianna on her back.

A minivan with an illuminated taxi sign on its roof emerges along the beach. Its wipers are turning intermittently. The driver notices Vanessa Cox under the weight she's carrying, along with the other two men following her in tow. So instead of waiting for them to flag him down, he takes the initiative by stopping to give them a lift. The taxi driver, shouts through the rolled down window on the front passenger side of the taxi, as rain pours in drenching his leather seat.

"You people look stranded. Where are you heading to?"

Bill Levy answers,

"Gosh, anywhere out of this rain. We are soaked!"

Taxi driver replies,

"That's okay! I have leather seats!"

They get ready to board the taxi.

"Great! The closest hotel would be fine."

Vanessa says.

"Let's do it! Thanks, cabby."

Coles says.

The taxi driver gets out and activates his umbrella to assist the stranded passengers with their boarding.

The cab driver gets ready to board. Levy, leaving nothing up to chance caps the Good Samaritan cab driver.

"Why did you do that?'

Asks the water drenched Brianna.

"He's too nice. He must have a hidden agenda."

Replies Bill Levy,

"Really?"

Asks Brianna.

Bill Levy ignores the nine-year-old little girl's questions.

"Be a quiet little girl, stop being a wise kid."

Says Vanessa.

"Just like her dad. The apple doesn't fall too far from the tree,"

Says Bill Levy as he drags the corpse into the water.

"Load up let's get out of here."

He continues.

They quickly load up the taxi with their sacks of money. Levy leads the way as he jumps inside the taxi and takes the wheel. The others board expediently.

The taxi departs and slides in the sand as it takes off. They leave the beach hastily.

21

THE RAIN TAPERS OFF as the taxi pulls up at the Bermuda Hilton. Vanessa Cox grabs her bags off the rear seat next to her and is the first to jump out dragging Brianna with her. Before Bill Levy could get out of the driver's seat, Vanessa turns to both him and Coles and says:

"Have nice life guys. It was great knowing you."

Coles and Levy look at each other in amazement; they are taken aback as Vanessa and Brianna depart inside the reception area of the hotel. Her two partners in crime are frazzled. The two men re-board the taxi. For a while, there is a stretch of silence between these two partners in crime. Suddenly, Bill Levy breaks the silence,

"So where do you want to be dropped off?"

"Drop me off at Hertz Rent a Car."

Says Coles.

"Man you know I can't do airports. Our pictures could be plastered in every terminal and Men's room in that joint."

"There's got to be an offsite location on this island."

Says Robert Coles as he accesses the navigation on his I-phone. Moments later, he locates a local Hertz office. He notices his watch.

"Well …"

Says Coles,

"What's wrong with you? You've changed your mind?"

Interrupts Bill Levy,

From across the street, it is clear to Robert Coles that the office is closed as the lights are out. However, there are cars on the lot secured by a barbwire fence.

Robert Coles thinks about stealing one but changes his mind.

"I'll wait until they are open. Those bastards are still asleep. Where is their graveyard shift?"

It begins to rain harder.

Bill asks,

"You are sure about that?"

"Yes."

Replies Coles.

Levy looks at Coles,

"Don't tell me you've never stolen a car in your life."

"Never!"

Says Coles.

"You just robbed a bank, what difference does it make…"

Says Levy.

Coles has heard enough.

"Wait here."

Says Coles, heading towards the fence,

He looks at the barbwire, and in his mind sees the type used to secure prison compounds. He makes a beeline to the taxi.

"Pop that trunk open!"

He says to Levy.

Inside the trunk, he discovers a tool box. He opens it and discovers among them an assortment of tools, a heavy-duty pair of pliers, and a slim-Jim. Coles returns to the fence and cuts away at it. He now has access to the lot.

Soon he is sitting under the driver's seat of a Peugeot. He hot-rods it and is now mobile. He picks up his bags of cash from inside the taxi and says to Bill Levy, "Your number is saved in my I-phone."

The two partners in crime shake hands in the rain.

22

LATER, THAT MORNING the news breaks not only about the abandoned ship, which ran ashore but also about the Hertz lot. The Bermuda police race down to the beach as well as to the car lot in investigative pursuit.

The once beach going community is now a lock down crime scene with yellow tape and cones. Many nosey villagers still try prying their way in order to get the 411 on last night's events.

Moments later a veteran detective Arthur Miller shows up in a Peugeot. The detective is African American decent in his mid-50s.

Miller goes aboard the ship which rests upon its side close to shore. Inside the vessel, he discovers no one. Additionally, Miller searches for fingerprints and begins lifting them from multiple surfaces. He then traces footprints in the sand on the beach. He measures them accurately. A stench draws his attention to the body of the taxi driver now washed up onto the beach. He yellow tapes the area and departs. Medics arrive later and transport the corpse.

Moments later, as the news continues to spread about the fiasco, a crowd gathers and thickens. The beach is now cluttered mostly with photographers, news media, onlookers, and gossipers. Many walk away with unanswered questions about a crime too large for such a small community; an American crime too big for their small island to handle.

BACK IN LOS ANGELES, CALIFORNIA detective John Croft works out vigorously to rehabilitate his leg. His cell phone rings. He gets it on the third ring. "Hello, this is Croft."

He greets.

"Mr. Croft, this is detective Arthur Miller from the Bermuda Police Force. A ship ran ashore on the island early this morning. I was rushed to the scene and after my investigation, the fingerprints of your daughter Brianna were discovered in the hull of that ship along with those of Vanessa Cox, Robert Coles Bill Levy, and others unaccounted for, in this crime."

"Did you find her?"

Asks Croft,

"Find her?

Replies Miller,

"Do you have my daughter detective Miller?"

"Not as yet Mr. Croft. Although her fingerprints were found on the abandoned ship, her footprints were not discovered in the sand on the beach. Even so, we traced and validated the footprints of the three bank robbers. However, none of your daughters'"

"Are you sure her footprints weren't there?"

Croft questions,

"No sir. According to the specs on your missing daughter, her feet fit a size five shoes of medium width. None of the footprints matched hers. We will continue to investigate the tragedy and update you with our findings."

Miller states.

"Thank you, detective. Where can you be reached?"
Asks Croft.

"At the Bermuda Police Department."

"Thanks, detective."

Replies John Croft as he rushes upstairs and immediately begins packing his luggage.

Elizabeth emerges out of the laundry room and into the bedroom, first, she notices John's gun on the dresser.

"Honey, where are you heading?"

Thinking that John was inside the bathroom, she accidentally bumps into him coming out of the closet attired with his bullet-proof vest.

"To Bermuda! They discovered Brianna's fingerprints inside a ran-ashore-abandoned-ship, yet, there is no trace of her. The footprints of Cox, Levy and Coles were tracked on the beach, no additional evidence of our little girl."

Elizabeth interjects,

"But honey you are…"

The house phone rings. Croft grabs it.

"Croft, this is Lieutenant Davis."

"Speak fast Lieutenant."

Croft suggests.

"I have been briefed on the situation in Bermuda surrounding the kidnapping of your daughter.

Knowing that you are still getting your strength back, we would be willing to send in several of our men to try to find her."

The Lieutenant says,

"Thank you, sir, but I've got this,"

Croft says as he puts on his vest.

"You understand that you are crossing the Atlantic, where, not only the culture is different but their laws are not as stringent."

Lieutenant Davis reminds,

"Davis, I hear you. However, 'Blood is thicker than water.' It is my responsibility to find my daughter, not yours, nor the BHPD, the FBI, CIA or the government of our country. It's my responsibility to find her."

Croft says as he put his gun in its holster.

Outside his house, a taxi cab pulls up.

"The woods are lovely, dark, and deep, But I have promises to keep, and miles to go before I sleep,"

Croft says as he hangs up the phone.

He kisses his wife along with two daughters, who are now engulfed in tears.

Croft is out of the door.

He boards the taxi.

Taxi takes off to the helicopter pad. Croft boards a chartered helicopter bound for Bermuda.

23

THE HELICOPTER TOUCHES DOWN in Bermuda. John Croft disembarks. He says to the pilot: "I'll call you when I'm ready." He is focused. Moments later, he takes off in a sedan. He calls Detective Arthur Miller's number and gets a busy tone. He tries again a few minutes later and gets the same results. He is not happy and feels like he has been conned into the whole Bermuda trip. Upon conducting a background check on Miller before leaving the States, there wasn't much disclosed except he worked for the Bermuda Police Department. His status was single and never been married, and he specialized in water-related cases.

Croft, knowing how bad things have gone within the last year wanted to make sure he didn't get sucked into an unwarranted situation with Miller. He questioned if Miller was really the guy he said he was, and if he had really recovered fingerprints of Brianna on the abandoned ship. Additionally, why wasn't Miller accessible now that he had landed in Bermuda to meet with him?

Croft decides to conduct his own investigation at this point. So he readies himself and drives to the location where the alleged ship ran ashore. There he sees the ship roped off and protected and secluded from the public. So he reverts to taking pictures of what seemed to have been or about to be transformed into a museum. While doing so he collects hair samples which he sent to the crime lab. This DNA later turned out to be Brianna's.

Again, he calls Miller. This time, he gets a dial tone. Miller picks up on the second ring.

"Hello this is Detective Miller,"

"Detective, this is John Croft. I am here on the island and wanted to see if we could get together to discuss some of your findings. I visited the ship but realized that it was off-limits to the public."

"I see. They let no one close to that thing. Let's meet tomorrow for breakfast at Chick-Fil-A, close to that beach at 9:00 a.m."

Miller instructs.

"I will see you then."

It is almost nightfall. Croft leaves his hotel, gets into his car and drives to the beach where the ship resides. He pulls up next to the shed where earlier the bank robbers boarded the taxi.

Croft notices a short guard, of African American decent gait up and down the beach, and waving his baton. Their eyes meet.

"Sir, how may I help you? Didn't you read the sign? It says no visitors allowed."

States the guard.

"I may have missed it. Sir, I would someday like to own that ship if it's for sale and just wanted to take some pictures of a ship which could one day become a museum."

Croft replies,

"There is too much crime attached to that ship."

Says the guard.

"Really? My little girls would love some of those pictures. Do you have kids?"
Inquires Detective Croft.
The guard smilingly says,
"Yes! Three girls, 6, 9 and 12."
And you?
"Three girls."
Says Croft.
The guard breaks down sobbing as he sheds a tear. Regaining his presence of mind after drying his eyes he says:
"Go ahead; just don't get me into any trouble if you get caught."
"Thanks,"
Says Croft as he sticks a hundred-dollar bill in the guard's hand.
Croft boards the ship. Inside he cleans his foggy camera lens with his handkerchief. Croft not only takes a plethora of pictures but collects many fingerprints along with hair samples. It is now nightfall. He leaves.

24

VERY EARLY THE NEXT MORNING Detective Croft leaves his hotel and meets with detective Arthur Miller. The restaurant Chick-Fil-A is known as the joint where many of Bermuda's professionals meet for business breakfasts. The two men sit down for the first time since their initial conversation after the ship was discovered on the Bermuda shore.

"It is great to meet you in person Mr. Croft. I am sorry about the tragedy which you are confronted with. However, I must let you know that the Bermuda Police Department, as well as the Government of Bermuda, will do everything in its power to assist in the finding of your daughter Brianna."

Miller states with compassion.

"Thank you! Brianna is the apple of my eye."

Replies Croft.

Miller opens his attaché case and pulls out a folder. In it are several pictures along with notes on a notepad. Miller describes each of them. The ones with the footprints on the beach were at the bottom of the stack. Croft views intently no doubt looking for a glimpse of evidence pertaining to Brianna. However, there is none.

Miller senses the intensity in which Croft views the photos, especially those, taken with the footprints on the beach. So he quickly puts the pictures back in the folder and into the briefcase, securely closing it. Miller feels like he has been given a case not only with merit but one with high publicity. He is very knowledgeable that Beverly Hills where Croft is stationed is one of the wealthiest cities on the planet. So, to him, every bit of evidence collected is not only newsworthy but of tremendous value. If he could pull off a win, he could see multiple feathers in his hat.

Miller hands Croft his business card and adjourns the meeting.

"Call me if you need any help while here on the island,"

Says Miller.

"I feel as though I am back where I started when I arrived."

Croft says this, upon realizing that he is not going to get much support from the Bermuda Police, at least through Arthur Miller.

Miller's cell phone echoes. It is a text message. He reads it.

Miller says,

"Sorry, I could not be of more help. I've got to go. This ship is causing a sore eye."

Croft decides to pay a visit to the BPD himself. When he arrives, he is directed to speak with Basil Jackson, assistant to the lead detective Mike Green.

MOMENTS LATER, MILLER revisits the abandoned ship He notices a handkerchief on the floor inside the hull. He picks it up and examines it. The initials J.C. stands out. Miller confiscates the evidence and clues in that Croft could have been tampering. He takes additional pictures and leaves. Miller waves goodbye to the guard upon exiting the beach.

Miller visits the police barracks where he reports his findings to the Bermuda Police Department. Upon arrival, he is informed that Detective Croft met with Basil Jackson, the assistant chief detective. Additionally, Miller drops off the handkerchief as proof to the tampering with evidence.

It is mid-afternoon; Croft is in the gym rehabbing his leg. His phone rings he aborts his workout and grabs it.

The voice on the other end is that of Mike Green, a head detective from the Bermuda Police Force. He introduces himself.

"Mr. Croft, I missed meeting with you today. I was informed my assistant Basil Jackson addressed some of your concerns. Additionally, your handkerchief was recovered earlier today at the scene of the abandoned ship on our beach. We ask that you refrain from the tampering of evidence regarding that ship. Although we empathize with the disappearance of your daughter, you must allow us to conduct this investigation as we see fit. You must understand that the ship is the property of the BPD."

John Croft is mute and taken aback as he returns to his work out.

Later, that day he hits the streets. Perusing village after village inquiring as to if anyone has seen his daughter. One woman in her 40s was so abrasive she tells Croft that if she found the little girl, she would keep her. Many refuse from assisting him by not providing him information, which could lead to reuniting him with his daughter Brianna.

The following morning, the police department issues a reward of $50,000.00 U.S. for anyone who turns in any of the three bank robbers, Vanessa Cox, Robert Coles or Bill Levy. On the other hand, if they turned in all three, the reward would jump to $200,000.00 U.S. Every police vehicle displays the message on a bumper sticker.

Many are confused about the multiple rewards. However, at many barber shops throughout the island of Bermuda, the talk is now about whose vehicle is better equipped to seek and find these three bandits. Some have even placed bets on who will turn in these bank robbers.

25

BILL LEVY ESTABLISHES A NEW identity using the name Aaron Schultz. Vanessa Cox already established the name Tess Shoemaker. Meanwhile, Robert Coles names himself alias Michael Frazier, all names fit in well with the islands. Additionally, Bill Levy alias Aaron Schultz purchases an immaculate house, perched above one of the most beautiful caves in Bermuda. It is privately gated, with a courtyard, high vaulted ceilings, a huge bar, oceanfront decks for entertaining, and four massive bedrooms. Guest quarters separate from the main home, with a living room, dining room, and bath. The house sports a three-car garage, with parking for three more cars off-street. Although it's not quite his ideal island home, it is fit for entertaining.

Meanwhile, his partner Robert Coles known as Michael Frazier purchases a beautiful beach house in a very secluded chic community on the northern end of the Island.

Bill Levy is still getting acclimated to his new home. While on the deck; getting his tan; his cell phone inside the living room rings. He rushes to get it. On the other end is Robert Coles.

"Hey Bill, I just wanted to let you know that there is a deal under the table for fifty acres. Do you want in on this awesome deal? It starts off at the lowest bidder. I also have a connection for potted plants. The auction is at noon tomorrow. Can you make it?"

Levy replies,

"Sorry Coles, I don't care for growing any crops. I've decided to stay clean. FYI, I learned that Croft has arrived at the island. Whatever you do, don't tell anyone of my whereabouts. All the best to you buddy. Levy hangs up the phone. He moves to his terrace and looks across at the Atlantic Ocean. He can taste the salty air. A fine sexy woman moseys out of the kitchen carrying two beers. She joins him on the deck.

"Aaron, you okay?"

She asks.

"Doing great!"

He replies.

The woman positions herself and begins massaging his neck and shoulders.

"Who was that?"

She asks.

His name is Michael Frazier. He wanted to know if I was interested in some marijuana farm land. I told him, I don't do narcotics."

In Bill's mind, he would rather separate himself from Michael Frazier and Tess Shoemaker. He can't let go beyond the fact that Tess has not been seen or heard from since they dropped her off at the Bermuda Hilton. Even so, Bill is very comfortable in his own setting, enjoying his privacy.

In the meantime, Al Peyton owner of the chop shop where Cruise 150 was refurbished shows up on the island of Bermuda. It was said that he met with Robert Coles one day over coffee.

Additionally, Al Peyton, oblivious to Coles had been running from the law in California. When the news broke that Al was operating an illegal chop shop involved in stripping at least 20 cars per week and sending their parts to Mexico and Puerto Rico, Al Peyton bolted fearing he would get caught.

He picked Bermuda because he felt that the relaxed atmosphere was more to his liking. By this time, money for him was not a big issue. He just wanted his peace and quiet.

One night he ran into Robert Coles at a party, where if it can be rolled, they smoked it. Robert never explained to Al that he had changed his name. So Al called him Rob. Al knew completely that Robert, Bill, and Vanessa had pulled off the bank robbery in Hollywood, but they never discussed it.

One thing Al knew for sure is that the car he refurbished was involved in the getaway, taking law enforcement officers from multiple agencies in a high-speed chase from Hollywood to Malibu.

26

BACK AT THE HOTEL ROOM, John Croft spends most of his morning inquiring about recent real estate sales and rentals conducted on the Island of Bermuda within the past six months. Nothing comes up with the three names: Vanessa Cox, Bill Levy or Robert Coles as homeowners. Additionally, nothing comes up linking them to any rental property.

Fed up, Detective Croft revisits documented information on all the purchases and rentals made during that month and recorded by the Home Buyers Association. He feels they would at least have that much-needed information. The highest purchase was made by an entrepreneur Aaron Shultz, according to his extended search and info gave by an inside source at the HBA. So Croft decides to pay Schultz a visit to find out if he was in any way connected with the bank robbery.

Detective Croft inputs Shultz's address on his GPS and heads out to the gated community.

Moments later, the Bermuda Police Department which tapped into the phone line at Croft's hotel room, transfers the info gathered from Croft's conversation with the HBA inside source to their liaison Arthur Miller.

Immediately, Miller heads out to Schultz's residence. He pulls up at the service station and fills his car up with gas. In addition, he checks his wiper blades and even the oil level in the engine. He jumps in and hits the road.

On the other hand, John Croft is caught in the early morning, stop and go, city traffic en-route from his hotel.

Later, that evening at sundown, Miller arrives at the gated community where Schultz resides. He pulls up at the gate.

The GUARD is present at the gate.

The Guard asks,

"How may I help you?"

"I am with the Bermuda Police Department. I am responding to a domestic violence dispute."

Says Miller.

"That's news to me. Sir no one has reported such an incident. Are you sure that you have the correct address?"

The Guard replies.

Miller flashes his badge. Something he should have done in the beginning.

"Do you know that you can get arrested for interfering with police activity?"

Miller reminds the guard.

"Sir, with all due respect, I am here doing my job. No one has reported any such incident to our office. Therefore, I will not be able to grant you entry. This is a private community. You've not told me who you are visiting."

The confident Guard states.

"Shultz, Aaron Schultz."

Says Miller.

"But sir, he has not informed us that he is expecting visitors."

Says the guard.

"Schultz must have forgotten."

Says Miller.

The guard dials Schultz's unit and connects the live video feed showing Miller and his car.

Meanwhile, Bill Levy "aka" Aaron Schultz is tuned into the scene at the gate via his TV set, which is rigged to the front gate's control system. He notices as Miller steps out of his car, shoots the guard, and opens the gate. Schultz arms himself and waits.

Arthur Miller finally shows his badge and proceeds to Shultz's residence. He pulls up outside and readies himself to exit the car. Levy "aka" Schultz waiting at the partially opened window, sees him and releases several rounds on the Peugeot.

Miller goes to the floor, crumpled up. He is unscathed by the bullets which leave their evidence through the front passenger door.

Bill Levy alias Schultz opens the manhole in the ceiling of his house and retrieves a sack of money. He goes to his car, puts it inside the trunk, gets under the steering wheel and takes off armed.

Miller raises his head and notices as Levy tries to make his getaway. He starts up his car and pursues Levy at the full speed.

Meanwhile, Croft comes through the open gate to the house. He recognizes Miller's Peugeot. After a closer look, he realizes that Miller is pursuing Bill Levy, the driver in the other car.

Detective Croft makes a swift U-Turn and pursues both vehicles. It's the first-time Croft has seen Levy since the Malibu car chase which landed him in the hospital. Levy looks younger and seemed to have acquired a tan.

Levy's car, a red Ferrari makes it through the gates, followed by Miller's Peugeot. Croft's car, a squad type sedan makes its way through the gates in pursuit.

The three cars hit the streets at high speed. Luckily, the evening traffic has dwindled. Levy's Ferrari is taking them on a chase like no other. His car's exhaust sounds like that of a motor boat as it careens around the bends on the road.

Miller tries to keep pace and finds himself no match. Even so, Croft is now catching up to Miller. The vendetta against Croft looms large in Miller's mind, so he presses the accelerator to the floor in pursuit of the money man, Levy.

Miller had his mind set on turning in Schultz. Now with Detective Croft in the mix, his objective looks bleak. To make matters worse based upon the name change, Miller refers to the man in question as Schultz, while Croft only knows him as Levy.

The gap between Levy's car and Miller's widens while the gap between Miller's car and Croft's narrows

Croft would rather get Miller out of his way as he needs Levy alive. So he unloads several rounds on Miller's Peugeot. The Peugeot is now saturated with bullet holes, but it continues to pursue Levy's Ferrari.

The Peugeot begins gaining some yardage on Levy's car as the Ferrari runs into some late beach traffic.

Miller now triggered happy and unloads several rounds on the Ferrari. None of them connects as the swift automobile continues to leave the duo in its dusty exhaust smoke.

The Ferrari comes up on an intersection which is flooded with truck traffic. Nowhere to go it glides up on the embankment, avoiding that collision and eludes its two pursuers.

The intersection clears out as soon as Croft nears Miller's car. Detective John Croft is poised to eliminate Miller's car and Miller with his arsenal. He shoots at Miller.

Miller's acceleration, out of that debacle, puts him a great distance ahead of Croft. He is now in close proximity of Levy Ferrari.

Meanwhile, Miller shoots at Levy, who once again eludes him with velocity.

Croft's car is now tailing Miller's. Bullets once again rain on Miller's Peugeot from Crofts' onslaught. The Peugeot zigzags out of the gunfire.

Up ahead, Bill Levy's Ferrari begins to slow up.

Miller detects the now slower pace of Levy's car and speeds up. By doing so he avoids yet another close encounter by Croft's gun attack.

Up ahead the rear left tire on the Ferrari shows a sign of a blowout. As a result, the car wobbles and glides on the embankment to avoid a collision with a moving truck at the intersection. Smoke emits from its punctured tire and rim, as both rubs against the pitched road.

Suddenly, Miller closes in on Levy.

The Ferrari comes to a complete stop. Levy retaliates by firing back at Miller with a vengeance. Click! Click! Levy's gun is now empty. He tries getting out of the car but John Croft, foot racing to the scene, is closing in on him.

"Don't shoot!"

Croft yells out at Miller.

Levy tries to escape on foot. It is too late.

Miller seizes the opportunity and shoots Levy through the car window and in his chest. The car door opens. Levy shoots back at Miller and misses. Levy rolls over a few times. He gets up a few times and then collapses on the street of the lonely highway.

"Where is my daughter?"

Asks Detective Croft,

Levy looks up at Detective Croft and draws his last breath.

Miller looking for another victim and a chance to take over the case aims his gun on Croft. He is ready to shoot the detective point blank.

The agile detective Croft unloads on Miller sending his body, in the distance, and into the gutter on the other side of the road.

Croft investigates, ensuring that Miller is no longer alive. He shoots Miller a second time to make sure he doesn't have any chance of surviving the onslaught.

Croft searches through Levy's vehicle and confiscates a cell phone. Inside the glove compartment, Croft notices documents in Levy's car and confiscates them. He peers deeper inside and discovers a huge amount of cash. Croft throws the sack inside his car.

Croft puts on a pair of gloves. He takes Levy's gun and exchanges it with the gun which he used to shoot Miller and puts it in Levy's hand. Croft then takes Levy's gun and puts it inside his car trunk.

Croft gets inside his car and makes a U-turn, heading in the other direction. Up to the street and away from the scene Detective Croft pulls over. He retrieves the gun, digs a hole and meticulously buries it.

27

ON THE NORTHERN SIDE of the island, Robert Coles now Michael Frazier is not only heavily involved in the growing of marijuana on a huge plantation, but he also imports and exports antique cars laden with cocaine, heroin, and meth.

His growing business is very profitable as he enjoys a lavish lifestyle. So much that he rolls with two bodyguards. To him, this is the life he had always envisioned after retiring from law enforcement.

John Croft is at a rest area. He goes through Levy's documents and cell phone contact list. He finds Robert Coles number inside Levy's cell phone. So he calls him up.

Robert is at a pool party kicking it with some Honeys. His phone rings. He checks his caller ID and sees that it's Bill Levy.

He answers,

"Schultz, talk to me. What did you get? Are you ready to purchase some acreage? I am making a killing!"

The voice on the other end replies,

"Robert Coles, this is John Croft. Where is my daughter?"

Coles is not only speechless but confused. He aborts the call. One of the Honeys sensing his frustration comes over and rubs up next to him.

Coles clues in that Croft has accessed Levy's phone. He thinks about what else could have transpired during that acquisition. Moments later Coles prematurely wraps the party fearing Croft would show up.

Croft puts a tracer on the location of that cell phone's call recipient and comes up with Northern Bermuda.

So without wasting any time he heads north in pursuit of Coles.

THE NEWS ABOUT THE DEATH of Levy and Miller's surfaces and the Bermuda Police Force alleges that there has to be a third party involved, so they put out a BOLO (be on the look-out) on John Croft.

Later, that morning, Bermuda Police Officers swarm the hotel where John Croft stayed as a guest. After talking with management, they discover that Croft had already checked out the previous afternoon. So they hit the streets in pursuit.

On the other hand, Croft is oblivious that he is being sought after. The winding streets of Bermuda are not the same as in America. He realizes. However, he perseveres passionately.

A huge billboard featuring a daycare center with kids ranging from ages 9 to 15, hangs on four poles overlooking a busy street. Croft notices the advertisement but stares at it far too long. Thus, he loses his focus on the road. The light changes to red Not only do a young couple cross the street with an infant in a stroller, but Croft's vehicle unable to stop clips the front wheel of the stroller almost running over the child. His car comes to a stop in the middle of the intersection.

The couple is shaken up. A police officer in a parked cruiser at the same intersection intercedes. The police officer comes out with the intention of issuing Croft a traffic violation.

The officer asks,

"You do realize that you almost ran over that little child by running the red light? Driver's license and registration please, sir?"

Croft provides the officer with the documents in question. The officer returns to his cruiser and writes the ticket. Before presenting it to Croft, he calls for backup. Two speeding squad cars arrive. Two officers from the first car put Croft in handcuffs and shove him inside the cruiser. Two officers in the other car oversee the arrest from inside their car. The squad car drives away with Croft in handcuffs.

As the news of Miller's death and the unidentified man spreads, so does the arrest of Detective John Croft. Coles watching that evening news is elated to know that Croft can no longer be a threat. So far, Detective Croft's arrest has not been linked to the murders. However, Coles has a gut feeling that Croft has been stirring up trouble on the island. And, that he could be connected, in one way or the other, to those murders.

28

AT THE BERMUDA POLICE STATION, Croft gets cross-questioned by two veteran officers. Although the duo is able to place him at the scene of the crime, they cannot determine if he was there before Miller got shot or afterward. Croft does not admit to cutting down Detective Miller in antagonistic or in friendly fire. Plus there seems to be no evidence linking him to the crime.

Additionally, the seasoned officers at the BPD claim that Levy shot Miller and vice versa based on ballistics evidence. They knew that because of the award money, anyone would be after Levy, wanting him dead or alive, including Miller.

There was nothing to attach Detective Croft too. Croft leaves the police station unscathed. He flags down a taxi cab. Croft gets inside the cab. The driver is African American local and in his late 50s. Croft is in no mood to converse except getting back to his car and continue searching for his daughter Brianna.

On the other hand, the driver looking for small talk starts conversing with Croft. The driver complains about how tough things are with the current economy in Bermuda as if Croft has the answer to the problem. Then he asks Croft.

"What brings you to Bermuda?"

Croft replies,

I am looking for a man and a woman."

"What are their names?"

The driver asks.

"I know everybody here in this town,"

He continues.

Croft senses that the driver is just looking for conversation, but Croft is centered on getting to his destination.

Hence, Croft replies,

"No, you don't. If you did they would be in the car with you right now."

The taxi driver takes an immediate timeout and goes mute until Croft gets to his destination.

Croft says,

"Pull over right here."

The car stops.

Croft pays the driver, who takes the money and returns the change to Detective Croft. The Detective says to the Cabbie,

"Keep the change,"

Croft hurries to his sedan and opening the driver's side door gets in quickly.

The taxi cab departs up the street with its driver unnerved and trembling like a leaf.

Croft gets into his car, starts it up and takes off in a hurry going the opposite direction. He emerges and takes the highway heading to Northern Bermuda. Continuing on that lonely highway, Croft notices a house in the distant valley. He pulls onto the road, accesses his magnifying glass, rolls down the window and zooms in for a close-up. From that elevated roadside, he gets a good look at the estate with a pool party in full swing. While the taste of that salty ocean breeze bathes his face and savors his mouth and lungs. He could hear music reverberating from poolside. No one he knows. They are all adults.

Croft is inclined to leave as he starts the car and rolls up the window. However, he changes his mind and zooms in for closer ups. This time, he picks up scenery worth its weight in gold Robert Coles meanders from inside the house and heads poolside with two chicks. Through his mind-sight, he could see himself reaching for his laser gun and toasting Coles. However, firstly, he is not armed with a laser gun, and secondly, he would rather corner Coles if he could and get answers from him regarding Brianna's whereabouts. Croft puts the sedan in drive and takes off heading in the direction of the house.

29

CROFT IS NOW IN CLOSE vicinity of Robert Coles' property. He takes in the scenic overlook and contemplates his move with both hands on the steering wheel and his car in motion.

Meanwhile, a call comes in from the Los Angeles Sherriff's department. Croft answers.

"Mr. Croft we wanted to get back with you on your daughter's disappearance."

"What do you have?"

Asks Detective Croft.

"We've checked with the FBI, CIA as well as other law enforcement agencies and nothing turned up positive in regards to her whereabouts." He is thus informed.

"Thanks, officer."

Remarks Detective Croft.

"What do I have to lose?"

Croft mutters under his breath.

The house is in a close range. Determined more than ever, Detective Croft drives his sedan directly through the front glass door and winds up poolside. The car stops short of nose-diving into the swimming pool. Partygoers run for cover as a result of the crash. So does Robert Coles.

It finally sets in with everyone at the pool party that this is nothing but a freak accident. So they begin to investigate in an attempt to assist the driver. Ahead of the pack is Robert Coles flanked by two armed bodyguards.

Out of the sedan steps Croft with his gun aimed at Coles. The bodyguards are aware that their boss is unarmed. Sensing that Coles is unarmed Detective Croft advises:

"Gentlemen you may want to hold your fire. This is nothing but a police investigation, and if you were to shoot at me, it would come down to he who shoots first wins. I know that you wouldn't want me to kill your boss who is unable to defend himself."

"Hell no; these are two against one!

Says one of the bodyguards.

Croft gets a closer aim at Robert Coles' head.

Croft reiterates,

"He who shoots first wins. I'm going for heads!"

"What do you want Croft?"

Asks Robert Coles.

"My daughter Brianna, if you don't have her, you are going to have to take me to her."

I have no information of her whereabouts,"

Robert Coles states.

The armed bodyguards stare at both men in wonderment as this saga begins to unravel. The guests now having something to chew on are digesting what's being served by this showdown. On one hand, the bodyguards know their boss as Michael Frazier. On the other hand, the man with the pointed gun is asking about his daughter's whereabouts and addressing Frazier as Robert Coles.

Robert Coles looks at the smashed car and then back at Detective John Croft his ex-boss.

Croft looks peripherally at the guests as they begin to leave the premises.

"Sorry, I can't help you. You are disrupting my party, Croft."

Says Coles as he watches his guests disappear.

With Croft's gun now in his left hand, Croft reaches inside his trouser pocket. He pulls out a set of handcuffs and throws them on the floor in front of the three men. They eye the cuffs with bigger eyes.

In the interim, Croft brings out another gun from under his coat and now have two guns pointed at Robert Coles and his men.

The remaining three onlookers/guests, who have just returned to check out the happenings move back, fearing their lives, would get snuffed out. It is now a four men stand-off, detective Croft against Robert Coles and his two bodyguards.

"Ask your men to drop their weapons, Coles."

Robert Coles looks to his right and then to his left. Both guards not completely trusting the man they have come to know as Frazier comply anyway.

With their guns now on the ground in front of Coles, John Croft, using one hand picks up one gun at a time and empties their bullets on the ground. Then he tosses both guns into the swimming pool.

"Down on your stomachs!"

Croft orders the guards.

Coles does not like this, but it's the only safe choice he has. The men comply once again. Croft cuffs Robert Coles. Then he checks to make sure that they are securely fastened. The other guests have not returned to the premises.

Croft is not trusting anyone caps the two guards.

"Let's move it Coles! I need to locate your car keys."

"Why my keys?"

Ask Coles.

"Because we are going to use your Ferrari,"

Says Croft.

"Nobody drives my car,"

Says Coles.

"Okay. We'll walk it then."

Coles directs Croft to where a variety of keys hang on a board in the kitchen. The board consists of keys for a Mercedes Benz, a BMW, Ferrari and a Dodge Viper. Croft grabs the set of keys to the Ferrari. He leads Coles to the garage where the black Ferrari sits independently of the other automobiles.

Croft opens the rear door, pushes the cuffed Coles inside and closes the door. He then gets into the driver's seat.

"Where is my daughter?"

Asks Croft.

"She is with Vanessa Cox."

"And where is Vanessa?"

Croft demands.

"Go out the driveway and hang a left and continue,"

Says Coles.

Detective Croft regards the driving instructions given by Coles.

Croft says sarcastically,

"Nice house!"

Coles does not respond.

Moments later, the Ferrari merges onto the elevated highway.

30

DETECTIVE JOHN CROFT and Ex-Cop Robert Coles turned bank robber; alias Michael Frazier; and the alleged kidnappers of Croft's daughter continued along that same lonely highway. Robert Coles is on the back seat handcuffed. He tries wriggling his way out of the cuffs to no avail. John Croft viewing Coles' intention in the rearview mirror states:

"I double checked it Coles."

Coles does not respond.

"So where is Brianna? I guess you thought you would never get caught, huh? Why would you want to hurt a little girl?"

Says Detective Croft.

"I was never involved in the kidnapping of your little girl,"

Replies Coles.

"… and you expect me to believe that?"

Questions Croft.

"… and if you weren't? Who is? And where is she?"

Demands Detective Croft,

"Vanessa took your daughter's custody after the shipwreck in Bermuda. She wanted your daughter Brianna ever since. That was her vendetta against you, not mine."

Reveals Coles.

"So where is Vanessa Cox now, waiting for your corpse to show up on her front lawn before handing over my daughter?"

Croft asks.

"No idea, I do not have a 20 on her."

Says Coles.

"You are a … liar! Always have been and always will be. You expect me to…,

Where is Cox?"

"I am taking you to her."

Croft wants to believe him but is still in a state of disbelief as Cole has not been definite regarding Vanessa's whereabouts.

"Who orchestrated her kidnapping?"

Asks John Croft.

"It was all Levy's and Vanessa's epiphany."

"So you expect me to believe that you had nothing to do with it? You just sat back and watched the fiasco all unfold. If you didn't why didn't you do something to prevent it?"

Croft counters.

"You expect me to put my life in jeopardy for your daughter's sake?"

States Robert Coles.

John Croft swerves the car from the left shoulder of the road to the right.

"What are you doing, trying to kill me?"

Asks Robert Coles.

"Yes! I will if I don't find Brie,"

Croft replies.

"Once again, where did you part company with Vanessa and my daughter after the shipwreck?"

Croft continues.

"Make a right turn here and pull into the next driveway to the hotel."

Directs Coles.

"Is that where Vanessa is?"

Asks Croft.

"This is where she checked in, and that is the last time I've seen her."

States Robert Coles.

Croft pulls into the Bermuda Hilton Hotel's driveway.

"They checked in here and that's the last time I saw them. That is the truth."

Say Coles.

Croft hurriedly exits the car with passion and purpose, leaving Coles behind still cuffed on the back seat. He surveys his surroundings as he saunters inside the hotel's lobby.

31

DETECTIVE JOHN CROFT enters the Bermuda Hilton Hotel and engages the assistant manager at the reception counter. He gets her attention. Croft flashes his badge. My name is Detective John Croft with the Beverly Hills Police department in California. I am looking for a woman by the name of Vanessa Cox. I understand that she checked in here recently. The woman checks on the computer. Then she informs Croft.

"I am sorry Mr. Croft, the guest in question Vanessa Cox checked out two weeks ago."

Croft asks,

"Were you the one who checked her out?"

"No sir, my manager I was off on that day. I believe my manager did,"

Answers the assistant manager,

The manager in the back office overhears the exchange of dialog and enters the front-desk area joining the conversation.

"I am Brad Miller, how may I assist?"

"My name is Detective Croft. I understand that you handled the checkout for a woman by the name of Vanessa Cox two weeks ago."

States Croft.

"I sure did."

Says the manager with compassion.

"Was she accompanied by a nine-year-old little girl?"

Asks detective Croft,

"She certainly did. The girl was crying. Her eyes were filled with tears when they left. She told her to stop her crying, and that she would get her the Barbie soon."

"Did she say where she was going?"

"No Sir."
Brad continues,
"Was that your daughter? We had no idea at the time that she was, sir. Alternatively, we would have contacted the Bermuda Police."
"Sorry, Mr. Croft."
Brad Miller says.
"If she checks back in, give me a call. Will you?"
Says Croft.
He gives the manager his card and leaves the hotel's lobby peeved.
Croft gets back in the car and slams the door hard.
Robert Coles in the rear seat waits for the next shoe to fall; it doesn't as Croft remains silent.
Time elapses. They have now left the hotel compound and merged with the traffic on the street without a word being spoken.
Croft finally breaks his moment of silence.
"You are going to need to provide me with more up-to-date information on your colleague Vanessa Cox."
"She's not there? I had no idea she left the hotel."
Says Coles,
"Yeah right!"
Replies John Croft,

At this point, Croft pulls over to the side of the road. He gets out. Then he opens the rear door and drags out the staggering Robert Coles.

Croft pushes Coles up against the car.

"Where does Vanessa hang out? I need answers now as he aims for Coles' head with his gun."

"Levy and I dropped Vanessa and your daughter off at that hotel. If you kill me, would that get you any closer to finding her?"

Vanessa said:

"Have nice life guys. It was great knowing you."

We were surprised that she was parting company seeing that we had just arrived in Bermuda, shipwrecked and none of us knew where we were going in a strange place.

We said our good-byes. That's how it all went down."

"So I guess I don't need you if that's how it all went down?"

Says Croft.

"Give me some more time I will see what I can come up with."

States Coles.

"Time I don't have. You need to understand Coles; I have a choice of picking up that reward money placed over your head by the Bermuda Police. I could turn you in or blow your head off myself."

Says Croft candidly.

"I will make some phone calls and see what I can come up with. However, I need some time. This is the Caribbean, not the U.S. Everything takes time."

Croft thinks it through.

"All you've got is 24 hours."

Croft opens the rear door and shoves Coles inside and gets in on the front seat. Croft turns to Coles and asks, "Whose number is up?

Coles doesn't get it.

Croft re-states,

"Whose number should we handle first?"

"Aren't you going to remove the cuffs?"

Asks Coles.

"Your corpse would look grittier wearing those handcuffs."

States Detective Croft.

"310-812-0101"

Says Coles.

"Whose number is this?"

Asks Croft.

"Vanessa's auntie,"

Replies Coles.

Detective Croft dials the number on his car phone. After three rings a woman answers.

"This is Gail Cox!"

"Gail, this is Robert, Robert Coles."

"Robert, how are you? I heard that you made it rich. Where are you?"

Questions Gail.

"Listen, Gail, I don't have a lot of time. However, I need to make contact with Vanessa. Have you heard from her recently or do you know of her whereabouts?"

Gail answers.

"If anyone should know where she is, it should be you, Robert. I love my niece, but I am not part of the in-game. I believe in the good cop philosophy. Since Vanessa hooked up with you and Bill Levy, her values went down the toilet. Her mother is rolling over in her grave right now with shame regarding the path her daughter has taken. If you see her tell her that Detective Croft has recovered, is out of the hospital and is looking for her..."

"Gail, this is detective Croft. I was informed that my nine-year-old daughter Brianna is in the company of your niece, Vanessa. Any information you could give leading to her recovery would be greatly appreciated."

Says Croft.

"I am so sorry detective. I empathize, but I have no information on your familial relationships. Robert, you should know better than to call me and not tell me that you are with the company. No wonder you are in the mess you are in – bad cop philosophy."

Replies Gail as she hangs up the phone.

Without wasting time, Croft asks,

"Who should we contact next? I need real connections; my daughter's life is at stake. See, you have no kids, never been married; you live the life of a gigolo. A Rastafarian Gigolo at that, growing acres upon acres of marijuana while importing meth and heroin. Brie is the apple of my eye. If we don't find her, I also know how to use a knife."

That last statement gets to the ex-police officer and bank robber.

"Why?"

Croft does not respond to Coles' question.

Because I am black?"

Retorts Coles.

"It has nothing to do with race. You can visualize it as black on black crime as much as you want. Those are the consequences you will face if Brianna is not found."

"Let's drive to the registrar's office."

Says Coles.

"Why?"

Asks Detective Croft.

"She could have changed her name."

States Coles.

"Why do we need to go through all of this, getting the government involved?"

Says Croft.

"On this island, people know you by your name. Without the right name, we are out of luck in finding your daughter."

Croft ponders.

Coles continues,

"But you are going to have to let me go in and talk to them."

"I am afraid that is not happening. You are going to have to come up with a different strategy. As a reminder, you only have nineteen hours left."

Croft relays,

"I am going to need to talk with my lawyer but in privacy."

Replies Coles.

"We are now down to the wire, and you have lost that right to privacy."

"Hey, man I am trying to help you find your daughter. Just dial the number, step out of the car and let me find some answers for you in privacy."

"Right now you are my prisoner and what I say goes. What is your next option before I ...?"

"Let's drive to the city of Hamilton."

States Coles.

Detective Croft reminds Robert Coles.

"Be sure this isn't a wild goose chase or else your remaining time is about to collapse."

32

THE DRIVING DIRECTIONS given to Croft by Coles, take Detective Croft into a downtown Hamilton alley. Croft pulls up into the alley. A Caucasian man named Al, who's in his 40s, emerges from inside an abandoned building. The look on his face indicates that he knows the car. Robert Coles signals to Croft to roll down the rear window. Croft anticipating hitting a home run accommodates, but he maintains a hold on the trigger of his semi-automatic.

Al moves closer to the rear door of the car.

"How come you are not driving your ...?"

He asks Coles.

Al somewhat startled upon noticing Coles sitting uncomfortably.

Al continues,

"Someone did you in?"

Coles pleads the fifth.

Upon breaking his silence Coles asks Al:

"Seen Vanessa lately?"

"Not since she picked up the Cruiser in Los Angeles ... Why?"

Al begins to put more of the dots together upon noticing the pointed gun in Croft's hand. In fear, Al retreats quickly back inside the building.

"Let's get out of here."

Robert Coles says to Detective Croft.

Before he could complete the alley exit, a car racing in the opposite direction gets his attention. Croft not only senses a head-on collision, he now imagines a total setup.

The Ford LTD with tinted windows is now closing in on him from that opposite direction in the alley. The driver manages to get a few rounds off at Croft's sedan while it speeds up in pursuit. Croft immediately shifts the car into reverse pursuant to making an escape.

Croft retaliates with some rounds of his own. The perpetrator would not let up, so Croft speeds away from that location driving his car in reverse. The Ford LTD is still in pursuit. Croft hangs a right. The other vehicle speeding out of control slams into an oncoming taxi cab and finds itself parallel to that vehicle but facing the opposite direction of Croft's sedan. Croft jumps out of his sedan in an attempt to waste the villain. The LTD takes off leaving Croft in its dust. Croft doesn't get even a glimpse of the driver.

In the interim, Robert Coles tries desperately to free himself from the handcuffs. But it is unsuccessful.

Croft re-boards his sedan quickly and is off in pursuit of the speeding LTD.

Inside the abandon building a mechanic toolbox along with miscellaneous mechanic tools and an engine, lift creates the aura of a mini auto repair shop. In the corner beside a used engine and other auto parts. Al is nowhere in sight.

Meanwhile, Croft continues his pursuit of the Ford LTD which has eluded him with the anonymous driver.

In the interim, the cab driver is enraged as he explains the hit-and-run accident to a Bermuda Traffic Police officer who is now on the scene. The overzealous officer calls for backup.

Moments later the streets are filled with police cruisers in search of the driver who left the scene of that accident.

A few miles ahead in a now desolate neighborhood, Detective John Croft continues to pursue that wanted driver. While on the rear seat Robert Coles cleverly tries to remove his arms out of those handcuffs.

33

THE PURSUIT OF THE FORD LTD by Detective John Croft continues except that now the Bermuda Police could also be on Croft's tail soon as indicated by sirens. Croft notices familiar driving habits by the targeted driver and in his mind questions the repeat of the chase in which he had to be airlifted to the hospital less than one year ago. Some things are different though the narrow curved streets, being in a strange country, the fact that one of the bank robbers is now sitting handcuffed in the rear seat of his car, he has not seen his wife Elizabeth and his two other daughters for over a month.

Suddenly, his cellular phone rings. He ignores it as he tries to keep up with the chase. Oblivious to him, though, it's his wife Liz on the other end. As a result of his apparent negligence Elizabeth is disillusioned and discontent. Her other two daughters wait with tear filled eyes for an update. She is unable to truthfully deliver. She just says:

"Daddy will find your sister."

The two girls trying to endure this long extended ordeal don't believe in anyone, anymore. To them, their sister's return is far from reality.

Detective Croft is now closing in on the Ford LTD. Also, fortunately for him the distance between him and the trailing Bermuda Police Officer cruisers has widened because of the rush-hour traffic buildup. They are as well in pursuit.

Coles sitting in the back seat and noticing the driving patterns of the driver being pursued knows that it could be none but the alias Tess Shoemaker. With all things being equal, he is uncomfortably being in this predicament.

Back in the alley two investigating police officers wait after sounding the warning:

"Come out with your hands on top of your head, or we are coming in."

Al finally comes out of hiding through a manhole from inside the building's ceiling. As soon as he steps outside the building in surrender, the Bermuda Policemen arrest him taking him into custody.

Prior to police surrounding the building, onlookers tell police that the car emerged out of the building and sped down the alley chasing a parked sedan. The witnesses tell the police that the sedan reversed its way out of the alley trying to avoid a collision and scattering bullets. After tracing the license plates Bermuda Police determines that the Ford LTD is registered to Tess Shoemaker at the abandoned building's address. An address shared with Al Peyton.

An outstanding warrant was out for Al's arrest in the US several weeks prior; for allegedly operating a Los Angeles chop shop. The two police officers put the cuffs on him taking him into custody.

Back on the streets, Detective Croft continues to pursue the driver who from her driving skills seems like the woman who is keeping his daughter Brianna hostage. In his mind, he weighs his options as shooting at the perpetrator could ultimately ruin his chances of getting Brianna back.

Croft continues to pursue the fast speeding Ford LTD. He tries to pass it on the right side on the open road of the two-lane highway. The Ford LTD narrows the passing room and cuts him off.

John Croft's sedan now finds itself several yards behind in the chase while the LTD speeds up.

Meanwhile, the two Bermuda Police cruisers keep weaving in and out of traffic with the aid of blasting sirens.

Back at the Hamilton Police Barracks two additional Bermuda policemen pull up outside and drag the handcuffed Al Peyton out of the cruiser and inside the station. They later book the chop shop operator.

Detective John Croft's cellular phone rings once again. This time, he checks the phone. In addition to the identified caller, his wife Elizabeth Croft, he notices a previously missed call from her.

He answers it.

"Hi Elizabeth, sorry I missed your call. I am in the middle of a high-speed chase and closing in on some answers. Let me get back to you. Tell the girls, I love them both."

Elizabeth hangs up the phone. In her eyes, she reminisces on that Malibu high-speed chase which ended in Croft being airlifted to the hospital when it all ended. Additionally, she relives the experience of seeing him hobbling around the house on crutches. The playback of these scenes agitates her.

By taking time out to answer that call, Croft is now further behind the steady speeding LTD, disappearing around the bend.

Looking at the gas gauge on the dashboard of the sedan Croft notices that the meter is reading close to empty. Robert Coles on the back seat notices the gas meter and reminds Croft:

"You are out of gas."

Croft gets the subliminal message in that remark and replies with a pointed gun towards Coles's head. He refrains, realizing that Coles could be the only lead to him recovering Brianna, even if he says that he knows nothing about his whereabouts. After all, Coles was an instinctive problem solver and negotiator at the Beverly Hills Station. He was great at making alleged criminals confess. In other words, he was great at digging, and he more often than not, found oil.

34

THE CHASE BETWEEN Detective Croft's sedan and the Ford LTD is still in progress. Now there's plenty of catching up to do. Detective Croft understands that speeding up the car will consume more gasoline. Plus with an eight-cylinder engine, the sedan can also be considered as a gas guzzler. Even so, the Ford LTD is still nowhere in sight, mainly because of multiple bends in that Bermuda stretch along the road. Croft speeds up anyway in order to catch up.

Moments later, Croft catches up to the speeding LTD on a long stretch of the open road. The LTD gains some control of the chase and hugs the road resulting in a successful speed away.

Now Croft has even more been catching up to do in order to match the speed of the disappearing LTD or even overtaking it. But can he do it when his sedan is almost out of gas?

Croft steps on the accelerator and succeeds in getting his car not only alongside and paralleling the LTD but for the first time he gets it close enough to steal a close-up look at the driver behind those tinted windows. He discovers that it is the woman who once worked for him; the driver from the getaway car to the scene of the recent Los Angeles bank robbery; and the alleged kidnapper of his nine-year-old daughter. Like Déjà vu, it dawns on him that he's involved in another high-speed chase with the same woman. His ultimate suspicion is now validated. It is Vanessa Cox.

Just when Croft is about to get a glimpse, of the passenger on the rear seat of the LTD, it speeds up. Vanessa with a gun pointed at Croft rolls down the window and shoots a few rounds off at Croft. Luckily, for him, she misses. That exchange causes Croft's sedan to slam against the Ford LTD and broadsiding it. Coles reacts to both the onslaught and then to the collision as he is tossed about on the rear seat unable to grab hold of anything for support.

To him if Croft changes his mind and lets him walk free the suffering endured has already amounted to more than he would have bargained for.

Prior to showing up at Al's place, which resulted in the chase, it had dawned on Coles how much Vanessa loved fast cars. Therefore, he aborted going to the registrar's office, also remembering that he himself is also endowed with an alias Michael Frazier. Instead, he decided to pay Al, a visit. He had no idea that Vanessa would be in that vicinity getting her speedster prepped. Now he realizes for sure that it is Déjà vu except that he is not inside the car with Vanessa under the wheel. All things being equal he would not have signed up for this expedition again.

Croft glances at the car's dashboard. The empty displayed gas gauge is not only more noticeable but the now illuminated light accompanying the apparent gas drought creates further concern for the detective.

Additionally, his adrenaline is at an all-time high realizing that the passenger in that LTD could be his kidnapped daughter Brianna. So he is all dressed up, so to speak, with the least possible distance he could entertain.

Detective Croft also realizes that not only is he in a race against time; knowing the reputation of the driver; however, that any wrong move made by him or Vanessa Cox could result in causing bodily harm to his daughter. So he keeps pace with the speeding LTD hoping that the odds will turn up in his favor. He reaches into his wallet inside his seat pocket. He takes out Brianna's baby picture, taken when she was only three years old and reflects as he keeps pace with the LTD.

35

THE CHASE NOW EMBARKS on a stretch of an unevenly pitched road. Not only is Detective Croft's sedan running on fumes, the car engages in a series of stop and goes movements. Croft realizes that for him, there is no pit stop.

Finally, he notices the Ford LTD slowing down also. Suddenly, the LTD comes to a complete stop at the side of the road. Feeling as though someone has granted him a favor, Croft pulls up his sedan behind the car but with some distance between. He puts the car in park and races down the downgrade towards the disabled Ford LTD.

Before he could get there, though, Vanessa jumps out from the driver's seat armed. She opens the rear door and expediently drags out Brianna. Brie has a rag tied on her mouth. She is wearing a black pair of designer jeans, a pair of white sneakers and a light sweater, which fits snugly on her.

Vanessa positions the nine-year-old in front of her, standing on an incline, using her as a human shield.

Brianna yells despite the tied rag in her mouth:

"Daddy! Daddy! Daddy!"

To the little girl, her dad is so close but yet so far, fearing that any moment death could separate them for eternity.

Croft is relieved seeing his daughter alive again for the first time in months but also knows that he only has one chance to get her back alive with a gun pointed at him. He is also mindful that he has to take out Vanessa Cox without causing any bodily harm to his nine-year-old daughter Brianna. So he tries negotiating.

"Drop your weapon Cox!"

Croft demands.

Vanessa Cox doesn't budge. Instead, she focuses on finishing off Croft with a shot through his head. She fires and misses.

"What do you want, Cox?"

Asks Detective Croft.

"You give her three and not even one for me. All I wanted was one, John."

Says Vanessa.

"We never had it like that, Cox,"

Replies Detective Croft.

"You are such a liar. Always been one. You are now out of miles before you sleep because the chips are stacked on my side. I have what you want."

Says Vanessa Cox as she shoots off another round at Croft. The bullet misses his left earlobe as he agilely dodges out of it.

Vanessa continues,

"Not only does your daughter know the other life you've lived. She hates you. She hates your guts."

"You have ruined my family enough Cox. Now drop the gun. Let's settle this. Give me what I want and take your money and run."

Says Croft as he fires one off mainly to get her attention.

Once again, Vanessa does not cooperate. She glances across the street at the immovable speedster.

"You are such a fake, Cox: Using fictitious names as Tess Shoemaker, kidnapping, bank robbery, and what else?"

States Detective Croft.

"You suckered me into the sketch of living a double life - Yours and mine. You made me believe repeatedly that you were into me. Our child could have been her age."

Replies Vanessa Cox.

Police sirens are now heard approaching in the distance.

In the interim, Robert Coles climbs over from the rear seat and positions himself under the driver's wheel. With the engine still running, on fumes and whatever gasoline remaining in the gas line based on the downhill positioning of the sedan enabling the downward flow. Coles uses his left shoulder to steer the car and his mouth to shift the car into the drive.

The car takes off downhill in Croft's direction on the other side of the street.

Brianna yells,

"Daddy, watch out!"

With the oncoming sedan, added by the site of the two fast approaching Bermuda Police cars Vanessa Cox loses her focus.

Croft shoots at her head and connects. Vanessa falls to the ground releasing Brianna from her arms as she collapses on the street.

Croft shoots at the moving sedan and blows out the front windscreen shooting Robert Coles in the chest. The car rolls over the embankment bursting into flames.

Brianna picks up Vanessa Cox's handgun. She aims it towards her dad.

"Dad she was right. You cheated on mom."

"What are you doing Brie?"

Asks Croft,

The two Bermuda Police cruisers are getting closer.

"All those nights when mom was home alone with us, you were with her. You were gone for days. You said you were working doubles; covering for anonymous officers. Mom needed you to be at home for me - Your little Brianna."

"Brie put down that gun! Please do as I say."

"But you were gone showing Vanessa a great time. You lied to us all along. Now I have the gun."

Brianna waves the gun.

Croft, not knowing what to expect is very cautious.

"So she brainwashed you, huh? Did she hypnotize you? You fell for it ... Brie?"

Brianna begins to cry.

The police cars are narrowing in.

She shakes nervously.

The gun falls out of her hands.

Croft grabs her in his arms.

The police car pulls up. The officers get out of their cars and approach Detective John Croft.

The Lieutenant in the group states:

"Mr. Croft, it seems like you have underhandedly accomplished your mission."

Now without a car, he looks towards the officers. They clue in.

The Lieutenant states:

"Mr. Croft before we leave I am going to have to write you up for such reckless driving, endangering the lives of others."

Croft looks at Brianna,

"How come?"

Asks Croft.

The Lieutenant replies,

"We clocked you driving 50 miles above the speed limit."

"Really?"

Asks Croft.

The Lieutenant replies,

"This is not the U.S."

RENEGADE COPS

Watch For The Upcoming New Releases…

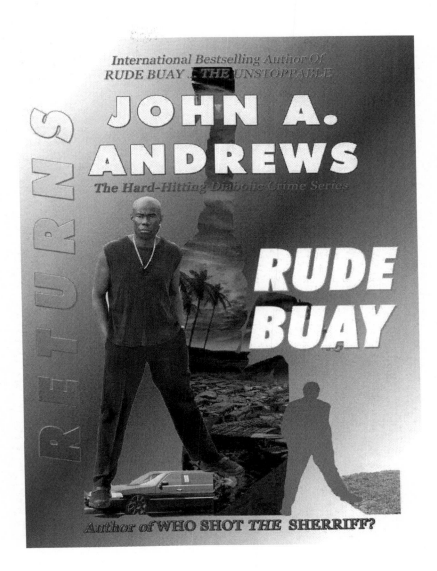

Other Favorite Titles

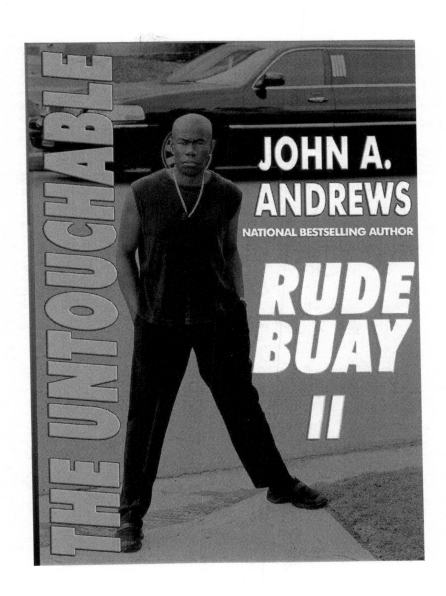

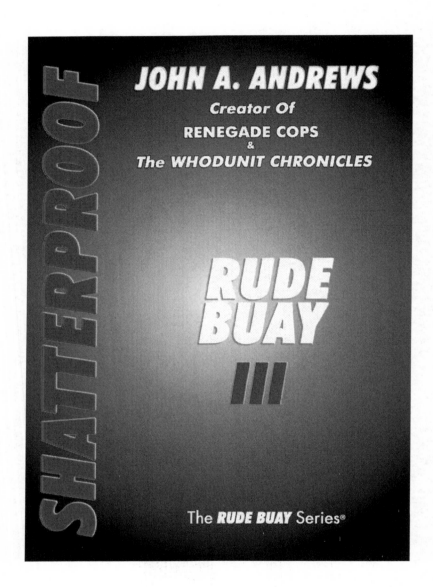

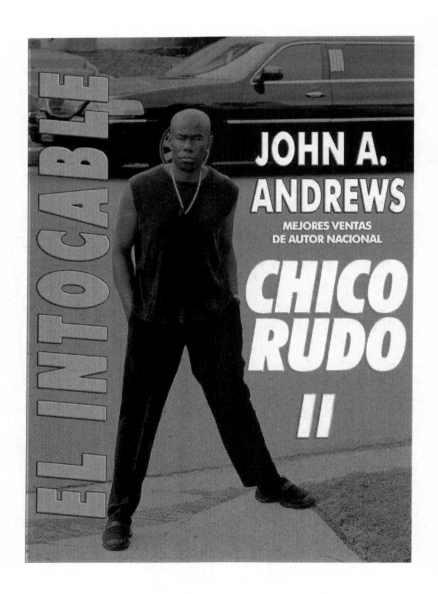

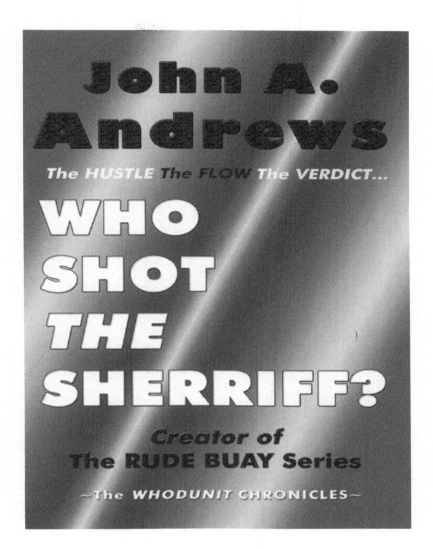

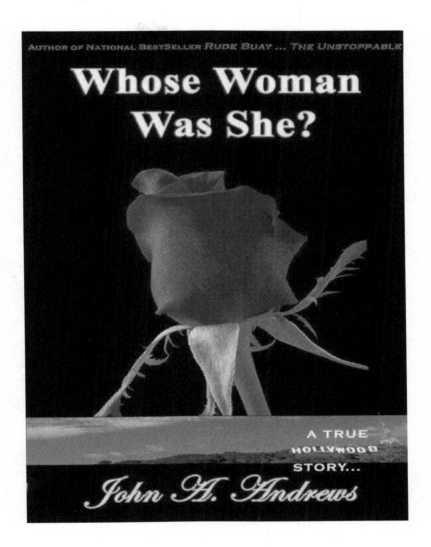

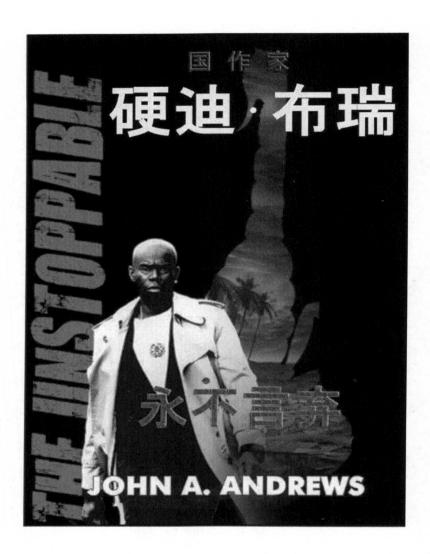

National Bestselling Author

Dare To Make
A
Difference

SUCCESS 101

JOHN A. ANDREWS

VISIT: WWW.JOHNAANDREWS.COM

Made in the USA
Charleston, SC
15 November 2016